PUFFIN BOOKS

Unbea

Paul Jennings was born in England in 1943 and emigrated to Australia aged six. The trip for the family cost ten pounds – the Australian government paid the rest of the fare in those days.

Paul taught disabled and socially deprived children for six years and then worked as a speech therapist. He later lectured in special education before his appointment as Senior Lecturer in Language and Literature at the Warrnambool Institute, where he worked for ten years before becoming a full-time writer in 1989.

Paul's stories are funny, weird, and wacky with surprising endings. He wants all children to have their noses in the same books and reluctant readers to discover that reading is fun. 'Books are fantastic. That's what I want my readers to think.'

Since *Unreal!* was published in 1985, Paul's books have sold over six million copies. He has won many 'Children's Choice' awards and in January 1995 was awarded the Medal of the Order of Australia for Services to Children's Literature.

PAUL JENNINGS

Unbearable!

PUFFIN BOOKS

PUFFIN BOOKS

Published by the Penguin Group
Penguin Books Ltd, 80 Strand, London WC2R 0RL, England
Penguin Putnam Inc., 375 Hudson Street, New York, New York 10014, USA
Penguin Books Australia Ltd, 250 Camberwell Road, Camberwell, Victoria 3124, Australia
Penguin Books Canada Ltd, 10 Alcorn Avenue, Toronto, Ontario, Canada M4V 3B2
Penguin Books India (P) Ltd, 11 Community Centre, Panchsheel Park, New Delhi – 110 017, India
Penguin Books (NZ) Ltd, Cnr Rosedale and Airborne Roads, Albany, Auckland, New Zealand
Penguin Books (South Africa) (Pty) Ltd, 24 Sturdee Avenue, Rosebank 2196, South Africa

Penguin Books Ltd, Registered Offices: 80 Strand, London WC2R 0RL, England

www.penguin.com

First published by Penguin Books Australia 1990
First published in Great Britain in Puffin Books 1994
15

Acknowledgement: The story 'Only Gilt' is loosely based on an urban myth
reported by Bettina Arndt

Typeset in Berkeley

Printed in England by Clays Ltd, St Ives plc

British Library Cataloguing in Publication Data
A CIP catalogue record for this book is available from the British Library

ISBN 0–140–37103–6

Contents

For my sister Ruth

Licked

Tomorrow when Dad calms down I'll own up. Tell him the truth. He might laugh. He might cry. He might strangle me. But I have to put him out of his misery.

I like my dad. He takes me fishing. He gives me arm wrestles in front of the fire on cold nights. He plays Scrabble instead of watching the news. He tries practical jokes on me. And he keeps his promises. Always.

But he has two faults. Bad faults. One is to do with flies. He can't stand them. If there's a fly in the room he has to kill it. He won't use fly spray because of the ozone layer so he chases them with a fly swat. He races around the house swiping and swatting like a mad thing. He won't stop until the fly is flat. Squashed. Squished – sometimes still squirming on the end of the fly swat.

He's a dead-eye shot. He hardly ever misses. When his old fly swat was almost worn out I bought him a nice new yellow one for his birthday. It wasn't yellow for long. It soon had bits of fly smeared all over it.

It's funny the different colours that squashed flies have inside them. Mostly it is black or brown. But often there are streaks of runny red stuff and sometimes bits of blue. The wings flash like diamonds if you hold them up to the light. But mostly the wings fall off unless they are stuck to the swat with a bit of squashed innards.

2

Chasing flies is Dad's first fault. His second one is table manners. He is mad about manners.

And it is always my manners that are the matter.

'Andrew,' he says. 'Don't put your elbows on the table.'

'Don't talk with your mouth full.'

'Don't lick your fingers.'

'Don't dunk your biscuit in the coffee.'

This is the way he goes on every meal time. He has a thing about flies and a thing about manners.

Anyway, to get back to the story. One day Dad is peeling the potatoes for tea. I am looking for my fifty cents that rolled under the table about a week ago. Mum is cutting up the cabbage and talking to Dad. They do not know that I am there. It is a very important meal because Dad's boss, Mr Spinks, is coming for tea. Dad never stops going on about my manners when someone comes for tea.

'You should stop picking on Andrew at tea time,' says Mum.

'I don't,' says Dad.

'Yes you do,' says Mum. 'It's always "don't do this, don't do that." You'll give the boy a complex.' I have never heard of a complex before but I guess that it is something awful like pimples.

'Tonight,' says Mum. 'I want you to go for the whole meal without telling Andrew off once.'

'Easy,' says Dad.

'Try hard,' says Mum, 'Promise me that you won't get cross with him.'

Dad looks at her for a long time. 'Okay,' he says. 'It's a deal. I won't say one thing about his manners. But you're not allowed to either. What's good for me is good for you.'

'Shake,' says Mum. They shake hands and laugh.

I find the fifty cents and sneak out. I take a walk down the street to spend it before tea. Dad has promised not to tell me off at tea time. I think about how I can make him crack. It should be easy. I will slurp my soup. He hates that. He will tell me off. He might even yell. I just know that he can't go for the whole meal without going crook. 'This is going to be fun,' I say to myself.

3

That night Mum sets the table with the new table-cloth. And the best knives and forks. And the plates that I am not allowed to touch. She puts out serviettes in little rings. All of this means that it is an important meal. We don't usually use serviettes.

Mr Spinks comes in his best suit. He wears gold glasses and he frowns a lot. I can tell that he doesn't like children. You can always tell when adults don't like kids. They smile at you with their lips but not with their eyes.

Anyway, we sit down to tea. I put my secret weapon on the floor under the table. I'm sure that I can make Dad crack without using it. But it is there if all else fails.

The first course is soup and bread rolls. I make loud slurping noises with the soup. No one says anything about it. I make the slurping noises longer and louder. They go on and on and on. It sounds like someone has pulled the plug out of the bath. Dad clears his throat but doesn't say anything.

I try something different. I dip my bread in the soup and make it soggy. Then I hold it high above my head and drop it down into my mouth. I catch it with a loud slopping noise. I try again with an even bigger bit. This time I miss my mouth and the bit of soupy bread hits me in the eye.

Nothing is said. Dad looks at me. Mum looks at me. Mr Spinks tries not to look at me. They are talking about how Dad might get a promotion at work. They are pretending that I am not revolting.

The next course is chicken. Dad will crack over the chicken. He'll say something. He hates me picking up the bones.

The chicken is served. 'I've got the chicken's bottom,' I say in a loud voice.

Dad glares at me but he doesn't answer. I pick up the chicken and start stuffing it into my mouth with my fingers. I grab a roast potato and break it in half. I dip my fingers into the margarine and put some on the potato. It runs all over the place.

I have never seen anyone look as mad as the way Dad looks at me. He glares. He stares. He clears his throat. But still he doesn't crack. What a man. Nothing can make him break his promise.

I snap a chicken bone in half and suck out the middle. It is hollow and I can see right through it. I suck and slurp and swallow. Dad is going red in the face. Little veins are standing out on his nose. But still he does not crack.

The last course is baked apple and custard. I will get him with that. Mr Spinks has stopped talking about Dad's promotion. He is discussing something about discipline. About setting limits. About insisting on standards. Something like that. I put the hollow bone into the custard and use it like a straw. I suck the custard up the hollow chicken bone.

Dad clears his throat. He is very red in the face. 'Andrew,' he says.

He is going to crack. I have won.

'Yes,' I say through a mouth full of custard.

'Nothing,' he mumbles.

Dad is terrific. He is under enormous pressure but still he keeps his cool. There is only one thing left to do. I take out my secret weapon.

4

I place the yellow fly swat on the table next to my knife.

Everyone looks at it lying there on the white tablecloth. They stare and stare and stare. But nothing is said.

I pick up the fly swat and start to lick it. I lick it like an ice cream. A bit of chewy, brown goo comes off on my tongue. I swallow it quickly. Then I crunch a bit of crispy, black stuff.

Mr Spinks rushes out to the kitchen. I can hear him being sick in the kitchen sink.

Dad stands up. It is too much for him. He cracks. 'Aaaaaagh,' he screams. He charges at me with hands held out like claws.

I run for it. I run down to my room and lock the door. Dad yells and shouts. He kicks and screams. But I lie low.

Tomorrow, when he calms down, I'll own up. I'll tell him how I went down the street and bought a new fly swat for fifty cents. I'll tell him about the currants and little bits of licorice that I smeared on the fly swat.

I mean, I wouldn't really eat dead flies. Not unless it was for something important anyway.

Little Black Balls

'What are these little black balls?' said Mum in a loud voice.

She was standing there holding a pair of my jeans in one hand and the little black balls in the other. I wasn't sure what to say. She wasn't going to like it. Mum usually checks the pockets before she puts my jeans in the wash. I should have emptied them. But I forgot. Now the jeans were all stained. 'Well . . .' I began.

'Come on, Sally' said Mum. She thrust the little black balls under my nose. 'Out with it.'

I just looked at my toes for a bit. Then I took a deep breath. It was no good stalling. 'Goat poo,' I said.

'Goat poo,' shrieked Mum. She threw the droppings on the floor and scrubbed at her hands with a towel. Then she turned on me with flaming eyes. I could

tell that she was just about to do something silly.
Like ground me for a month. Or stop my pocket
money.

'I can explain,' I said. 'You won't be mad when
I tell you what happened. Just give me a chance.'
I took another deep breath and launched into my
explanation.

2

See, I've got this friend. Everyone calls him the Paper
Man. He doesn't dress in clothes. He dresses in
newspapers. He wraps them around his arms and
legs and ties them up with string. In the winter he
wears lots of papers and in the summer he takes
some of them off.

The Paper Man doesn't believe in money. He's not
into buying things. He thinks everybody should get
by with a lot less. 'I don't need a car,' he told me.
'Or a house. Or a washing machine. I've got the stars.
And the cool wind off the sea. I've got the birds. And
the fish. I don't need television. Not when I can watch
the clouds tell a different story every day.'

This is how the Paper Man goes on. He doesn't
care what other people think. He has a mind of his

own. He lives in a bark hut on the edge of a cliff overlooking the sea. His carpet is paper. His bedcovers are paper. And his friends are the wild creatures that live on the cliffside.

The kids at school think he's crazy. When they see him wandering around in his paper clothes they call out names. From a safe distance of course. They pretend they want to buy a paper. Or ask him for fish and chips. But really they're scared of him. No one goes near his hut except me. I'm his friend.

I help him to care for the animals. He has a blind possum that he feeds every day. And a hawk that sits on his bed. It's a pet. A black hawk with a yellow beak. The hawk can fly off whenever it wants to. But it never does.

Anyway, yesterday I went to see him after school. He was sitting on a rock in the sun. On his lap he had a bag made out of old newspapers. I could see straight away that there was something moving inside.

'What have you got?' I said.

The Paper Man looked up with a sad smile. 'A friend,' he told me. 'A sick friend.'

I pulled back the paper and looked. It was a

beautiful little kangaroo. She stared up at me with soft, moist eyes. She felt safe in the arms of the Paper Man. He was strong and gentle. Animals knew that he would never harm them.

'Can you fix it?' I asked him. I thought I knew what his answer was going to be. The Paper Man had healed hundreds of animals. None of them had ever died.

He shook his head slowly. 'This one has bad trouble,' he said. 'It has a lump inside. It needs to go to a vet. For an operation.'

I knew he didn't like to go into town where people laughed at his newspaper clothes. 'No worries,' I said. 'I'll take her in for you.'

He looked up at me. 'That's really nice of you, Sally,' he said. 'But vets cost money. It's two hundred dollars for an operation. We have to get two hundred dollars.'

'I'll take up a collection,' I said.

He shook his head. 'It wouldn't be right. Not begging for money.' He walked into the hut and brought out a rusty old tin. He reached inside and took out something. It was a jewel. Small and lovely. It was smooth with blue and purple swirls running deep inside.

'An opal,' he said. 'My last one. From the old days. When I was a miner.'

I looked at the opal as it rolled around like an egg on his cracked, brown palm. Suddenly he took my hand. He opened my fingers and gave me the opal.

'Take it into town,' said the Paper Man. 'And sell it at the jeweller's. It's worth two hundred dollars. Cash it in for me. I know I can trust you, Sally.'

I went red in the face. No one else would have ever trusted me with two hundred dollars. People always say I lose things. That I'm a scatterbrain living in a dream world.

I stood up tall. 'I'll do it,' I said. 'But I won't be able to go to the jeweller's until after school tomorrow. The shops will be shut by now. And I can't wag school.'

The Paper Man's face crinkled up with a smile. 'That's the girl,' he said.

3

I walked back along the clifftop. The sun was setting into the sea like an ingot in a blazing furnace. A soft wind ruffled my hair. I looked at the opal and knew that it had cost the Paper Man a lot to part with it. I would never let him down.

Suddenly I heard something strange. At first I thought it was someone playing a joke. A sort of sad, bleating call. Then I heard it again. A baaing noise, like a sheep makes. It was coming from the cliff face.

I looked over the edge but couldn't see anything. There it was again. A loud baa. A cry for help?

The cliff fell dangerously into the sea. The water swelled and crashed below. The edge was rocky and crumbling but there was a narrow track down. I clasped the opal firmly and started to edge my way along, sitting on my bottom because I was too scared to walk.

I managed to inch my way around a clump of rocks and there he was. A large billy goat. He had a piece of chain around his neck which was tangled in a bush.

It was the dirtiest billy goat I had ever seen. Its long hair was matted with dung and dirt. It was covered in burrs and twigs. Its teeth were green and horrible. It baaed at me crossly.

'Okay, okay, Billy,' I said. 'I'll get you out.'

I was still sitting down on the little ledge, too

scared to stand. I pulled myself towards the goat carefully. The sea was a long way down. There were sharp rocks in the water. I hung on to tufts of grass with one hand. My other hand still clasped the opal. I was too scared to jam it into my pocket.

Finally I reached the goat. It wasn't a bit scared. The silly thing didn't even seem to know it was trapped. It started to nibble at my socks.

'Stop it,' I yelled. 'Stop it, you stupid goat.'

Billy kept on nibbling. He took a whole chunk out of my sock and swallowed it.

With my left hand I propped myself up so that I didn't fall. I tried to untangle the chain with my other hand. It was hard work because I was trying to hold the opal at the same time.

I felt the opal fall. It just slipped out of my fingers. It seemed to take for ever to hit the ground. It was as if it was in slow motion. I made a wild grab but the opal fell onto the track and rolled towards the edge.

Quick as a flash, the goat bent down and licked it up.

'No,' I screamed.

But I was too late. The goat gave a little swallow

and had the opal for dessert. It was gone. Buried deep in the blackness of Billy's bowels.

The goat had swallowed the Paper Man's opal.

4

The chain came away from the bush and Billy tried to escape. He shoved between me and the cliff. I tottered on the edge. If it hadn't been for the root of a dead tree I would have tumbled to my death. I hung on like crazy.

The ungrateful goat pushed past and bolted up the track. With the opal still in its belly.

I managed to crawl back up the cliff on my knees. I stood up and looked around. Just in time to see Billy clip clopping off in the distance.

I felt cold all over. I began to shake as I realised what had happened. The opal was gone. The goat was going. And the poor little kangaroo would miss out on its operation. It would die. And it was all my fault. I couldn't go back and face the Paper Man. I couldn't look into his trusting brown eyes and tell him that I'd lost his opal. The opal I was supposed to have sold for two hundred dollars.

The goat. I had to catch him. I belted after Billy

as fast as I could go. I tore along the clifftop. Billy was heading for town. Flat out. You might not think it but goats can run fast. I tried to keep up but I couldn't. My sides ached. I had a stitch. My lungs hurt.

I slowed to a fast walk. It was the best I could do. As I went I thought about the opal. How could I get it back?

I could take Billy to the vet's. I could offer him half the opal to operate and take it out. Or I could say, 'Operate on the goat and get the opal back. Then you can fix the little kangaroo and keep the opal. Two operations for one opal.'

But in my heart I knew he would just laugh. I was just a kid. And what if the opal had gone? Moved on, so to speak.

No, I had to catch that goat and get the opal back myself. But how? What goes up must come down. What goes in must come out. All I had to do was catch Billy and collect the droppings. Sooner or later the opal would appear in a little ball of poo. And everything would be all right.

Then I started to worry. How long would the opal take to complete its journey? Goats eat quickly. Maybe the opal would pass through before I could catch up with Billy. Slow motions wouldn't be Billy's style. I had to hurry.

5

I started to run again. I could see Billy munching some flowers in a garden just outside of town. This was my chance.

Boy, was I tired. But I kept running. Even with a stitch. Billy looked up just as I reached him. He broke into a trot along the footpath into town. He went past the shops. People stopped and laughed as he passed.

'Stop that goat,' I yelled at the top of my voice.

But no one did. Everyone thought it was a great joke. Billy ran across the road against a red traffic light. Then he stopped outside the chemist's shop. And did something.

'Oh no,' I groaned.

Billy ran on. I looked at the little black balls on the footpath. There was nothing else I could do. I couldn't risk leaving them there. One of them might have the opal inside. I picked up the pellets of poo and shoved them into my pockets.

You can imagine how I felt. There I was. On my

hands and knees in the middle of the main street. Picking up goat droppings in my bare hands. With everyone looking. I went red in the face. Then I jumped up and tore after the goat. How embarrassing.

Well, it was a terrible chase. Every time I caught up to Billy he dropped a few more pellets. I had to stop and pick them up. By the time I finally grabbed him my pockets were bulging with poo. And the people in the street thought I was crazy.

I walked slowly down the road, stopping every now and then to pick up Billy's latest offerings. Finally I reached home. I took Billy into the back yard and tied him up behind the garage where Dad wouldn't see him. 'Don't make any noise,' I said. 'This is a secret between you, me, and the little black balls.'

'Baaa,' said Billy.

6

That night I found it hard to sleep. I snuck out twice and searched around in the night with a torch. But no opal. Just more of the same.

In the morning I dressed for school. I found a

small cardboard box and borrowed a cheese knife from the kitchen. Then I went to check on Billy. He was gone. 'Oh no,' I groaned. I scooped up the new droppings near the fence and put them in a box. Then I followed the trail. Out through the hole in the hedge and down the lane. The pile in the box grew bigger. Finally I found him. His chain was tangled around a letterbox. The silly goat was munching away on someone's roses.

I didn't know what to do. If I tied Billy up he might get away again. And if the opal made an appearance someone else could find it. I thought of the little kangaroo. And my friend the Paper Man. I had to make the supreme sacrifice.

'Billy,' I said. 'You're coming to school.'

Well, talk about terrible. The first class was music. I sat there looking out of the window hardly singing at all. I could see Billy outside where I had left him. Chained up to a post on the school oval. He was straining on the chain. Looking towards me.

I had the box of goat poo under the desk. I hadn't had time to examine it carefully for the opal. I slipped up the lid and started cutting open the little black balls with the cheese knife. My hands were shaking with excitement. I didn't notice that the class had stopped singing. The silence was deafening.

Suddenly I realised. Everyone was looking at me. Shame. I tried to close the lid but my shaking hands let me down. The box fell onto the floor. The contents of Billy's belly scattered everywhere.

The kids laughed and jeered. They looked at me with disgust. I felt like a creep.

While all of this was happening, Billy had been busy. Goats are stupid things. It was lonely. It wanted to find me. It had broken free and was looking for me. Billy wandered through the front door and straight into the classroom.

'Who owns this goat?' yelled Ms Quaver.

Everyone looked at me.

'Sally Sampson,' she said. 'I might have known. What on earth have you brought a goat to school for? And what's that filthy stuff on the floor?'

I didn't know what to say. My head seemed as if it was going to explode. The kids were all giggling and laughing. 'I've got asthma,' I blurted out. 'I have to drink fresh goat's milk every hour.'

There was a long silence. 'You're not going to get much milk from a billy goat,' said Ms Quaver in a sarcastic voice.

The kids packed up. Talk about laugh. They rolled

around on the floor, helpless with mad mirth. Some kids held their sides as they hooted and cackled. I felt stupid. Caught out in a silly lie.

7

Ms Quaver pointed outside with a quivering finger. I grabbed Billy and took him back to the oval. 'Stay there,' I ordered. 'And don't let that opal drop until I come back.'

The class was singing some song about pennies from heaven when I returned. I had to clean up the mess in front of everyone. As I worked, I stared out of the window at Billy. He was eating and doing his business at the same time.

A feeling came over me. It was sort of like when you know that someone is looking at you. Like the time I threw an orange in the air just for fun. As soon as it left my hand I knew it was going to fall next door and hit our neighbour on the head. I just knew it was going to and it did. Well, I had another feeling like that.

I knew that Billy had finally dropped the opal. It was lying there on the grass. I just knew it.

A football team jogged out onto the field. One of

the boys untied Billy because he was in the way. Another boy with a large 2 on his jumper kicked at the goat droppings. Then he stopped and looked down. He bent over and picked something up.

I forgot all about the music class. And Ms Quaver. I rushed out the door and over to the oval. 'Hand that over,' I shrieked at Number Two.

'No way,' he said. 'Buzz off, little girl.'

Little girl. He called me little girl. I saw red. And I saw the blue opal in his hand. There was no time for talking. I grabbed Number Two's arm. The opal flew into the air. Up, up, up.

Then it started to fall. Way over the other side of the oval. It landed right between the goal posts. My opal almost landed on a bird that was searching for worms. A black bird with a yellow beak.

You might not believe what happened next. I could hardly believe it myself. The bird picked up the opal and flew off with it. It flapped right over our heads. I could see the opal clearly in its beak.

'Come back,' I screamed. 'Drop that opal.'

But it was no good. The bird flapped off towards the sea. I ran after it as fast as I could go. Billy trotted along behind. He stopped every now and then to nibble at a gate or some flowers.

What a day. Everything was going wrong. I puffed after the bird and finally caught up. It stopped for a rest by the beach and perched on top of a swing in the playground. 'Good bird,' I said. 'Good birdy. Drop it, birdy.' I tiptoed towards it.

Deep in my heart I knew it was hopeless. Birds don't come to you when you call. But I hoped that it might throw the opal away if I came close. I mean, why would a bird want an opal?

I could see the bird watching me with one beady eye. I crept closer. I reached up.

And the bird flew off. I watched as it flew out to sea, higher and higher. Then it opened its mouth and dropped the opal. It seemed to take for ever falling. A small speck plunging down. I didn't hear it hit the water but I saw it disappear. Way out deep. Where no one would ever find it. The opal was gone. Lost at sea.

'Rotten blackbird,' I shouted at the bird.

8

I turned and started walking towards the Paper Man's hut. What was he going to say? I had no opal. And no two hundred dollars. And the poor little kangaroo was dying and needed an operation.

Soon I was on top of the cliff, walking along a twisting track. I walked slowly. I didn't really want to get there. It was the worst day of my life. 'Baa,' said Billy. He was still following me.

'It's all your fault,' I said. 'Stupid goat.' I grabbed his chain and looked around for somewhere to tie him up. I'd had enough of goats for one day.

I found a tree by a small pond and this time fixed the chain very carefully. 'There's enough for you to eat here until I come back,' I said to Billy.

He stared back without saying anything. Trying to make me feel guilty. The way dogs do when you won't take them for a walk.

I trudged along the cliff with my head down. The poor little kangaroo. Now it couldn't have the operation because we didn't have the two hundred dollars. What if it died?

I had ninety-five cents in the bank. That was no good. I could ask for my pocket money in advance. I tried it out in my mind. 'Dad,' I could say. 'Will you let me have the next one hundred weeks' pocket money right now?'

The answer would be 'no' with a long lecture to follow.

By now I could see the Paper Man's shack in the distance. I stopped. I just couldn't tell him. My feet refused to move.

'Excuse me,' said a voice.

I just about jumped through the roof. Except there wasn't any roof.

I turned around and saw a man with a worried look and a bald head. 'Have you seen a goat?' he asked.

'A goat?' I replied.

'Yes, a Kashmir goat. With long hair. I brought it out from India. But it's run off. It's worth fifteen thousand dollars.' He hung his head and shook it in despair.

Then he looked up and said something that was music to my ears. 'There's a two hundred dollar reward for whoever finds it.' He took out two one hundred dollar notes and waved them in the air.

I gave an enormous smile. Then I grabbed the money. 'Follow me,' I said.

Well, that's just about the end of the story. I took the bald-headed man to Billy and the little kangaroo to the vet's for the operation. The Paper Man was rapt. I've never seen anyone as happy as he was when the kangaroo came back. She made a complete recovery.

9

Mum was standing there, still holding the jeans with goat-poo stains on the pockets. She had a soppy smile on her face. The sort of smile people have when they see someone's new baby. It was the type of smile that Mum rarely gave me any more.

'Why, Sally,' she said. 'What a lovely story. How sad. You kind girl. What a terrible time you've had.' She looked at the little black balls on the floor and the dirty jeans. 'Don't worry about the stains. Just clean up the mess and we won't say any more about it.'

I gave her a big smile and ran up to the kitchen to get a brush and dustpan. Dad was there. He was just going to open the fridge and get a beer. 'Don't,' I screamed.

But it was too late. He opened the fridge door. There on the top shelf was a little mouse. Sitting up on a saucer, begging. A dead mouse all covered in mould. It looked lovely. As if it was a polar bear wearing a long white coat.

Dad didn't think it was lovely. He stood there quite still. He didn't even turn around. He spoke slowly with a really mean voice. 'Sally, did you put this disgusting thing in the fridge?'

He turned on me with flaming eyes. 'Come on, Sally,' said Dad. He thrust the saucer under my nose. 'Out with it.'

I could tell that he was just about to do something silly. Like ground me for a month. Or stop my pocket money.

I took a deep breath and tried to think of another good story. Fast.

Only Gilt

The bird's perch is swinging to and fro and hitting me on the nose. I can see my eye in its little mirror. Its water dish is sliding around near my chin. The smell of old bird droppings is awful. The world looks different when you are staring at it through bars.

Fool, fool, fool.

What am I doing walking to school with my head in a bird's cage?

Oh no. Here's the school gate. Kids are looking at me. They are pointing. Laughing. Their faces remind me of waves, slapping and slopping at a drowning child.

Strike. Here comes that rotten Philip Noonan. He's grinning. He's poking bits of bread through the bars. 'Pretty Polly,' he says. 'Polly want a biscuit?'

I wish I was an ant so that I could crawl into a crack. Then no one would ever see me.

Teachers are looking out of the staff-room window. I can see Mr Gristle looking. I can see Mr Marsden looking. They are shaking their heads.

I hope Gristle doesn't come. 'Get that thing off your head,' he will shout. 'You idiot. You fool. What do you think you are? A parrot?' Then he will try to rip the cage off my head. He will probably rip the ears off my skull while he is doing it.

Mr Marsden is coming. Thank goodness. He is the best teacher in the school. I don't think he'll yell. Still, you never know with teachers. He hasn't seen a boy come to school with his head in a bird cage before.

'Gary,' he says kindly. 'I think there is something you want to say.'

I shake my head. There is nothing to say. It is too late. I am already a murderer. Nothing can change that.

Mr Marsden takes me inside. We go into the sick bay and sit down on the bed. He looks at me through the bars but he doesn't say anything. He is waiting. He is waiting for me to tell my story.

After a bit I say, 'All right. I'll tell you all about it. But only if you keep it secret.'

Mr Marsden thinks about this for a bit. Then he

smiles and nods his head. I start to tell him my story.

2

On Friday I walk over to see Kim Huntingdale. She lives next door. I am in love with her. She is the most beautiful girl in the world. When she smiles it reminds me of strawberries in the springtime. She makes my stomach go all funny. That's how good she is.

My dog Skip goes with me. Skip is a wimp. She runs around in circles whenever anyone visits. She rolls over on her back and begs for a scratch. She would lick a burglar's hand if one came to rob our house. She will not fight or bark. She runs off if Mum growls. Skip is definitely a wimp.

Mind you, when Mum growls I run off myself. When she is mad it reminds me of a ginger-beer bottle bursting in the fridge.

Anyway, when I get to Kim's house she is feeding Beethoven. Beethoven is her budgie. She keeps it in a cage in the back yard She loves Beethoven very much. Lucky Beethoven.

Beethoven can't fly because he only has one wing.

Kim found him in the forest. This enormous, savage dog had the poor bird in its mouth. Kim grabbed the dog without even thinking of herself and saved Beethoven's life. But he was only left with one wing and he can't fly at all.

Now Kim loves Beethoven more than anything.

I love Skip too. Even though she is a wimp.

Kim looks at Skip. 'You shouldn't bring her over here,' she says. 'Beethoven is scared of dogs.'

Skip rolls over on her back and begs with her four little legs. 'Look at her,' I say. 'She wouldn't hurt Beethoven.' When she rolls over like that Skip reminds me of a dying beetle.

Kim walks into Beethoven's aviary. She lets me in and locks Skip out by putting a brick against the door. Kim picks up Beethoven and the little budgie sits on her finger. It starts to sing. Oh, that bird can sing. It is beautiful. It is magic. A shiver runs up my spine. It reminds me of the feeling you get when fizzy lemonade bubbles go up your nose.

Kim puts the bird down on the ground. It is always on the ground because it can't fly. 'Tie up Skip,' says Kim, 'and I'll let Beethoven out for a walk.'

I do what she says. I would do anything for Kim. I would even roll over on my back and beg like Skip.

Just for a smile. But Kim hardly knows I am here. I tie up Skip and Kim lets Beethoven out for a walk. He chirps and sings and walks around the back yard. It reminds me of a little yellow penguin walking around on green snow.

Skip is tied up so she just sits and looks at Beethoven and licks her lips.

3

After a while Kim shuts Beethoven back in the aviary and puts the brick in front of the door. Skip sticks one ear up in the air (the other one won't move) and looks cute. Kim gives her a pat and a cuddle. 'She's a lovely dog,' she says. 'But you have to keep her away from Beethoven.'

'Don't worry,' I say. 'I promise.'

Kim smiles at me again. Then she says something that makes my heart jump. 'Next to Beethoven, you are my best friend.'

It is hard to tell you how I feel when I hear this. My stomach goes all wobbly. It reminds me of a bunch of frogs jumping around inside a bag.

I walk back to our place feeling great. Wonderful. Mum isn't home so I can let Skip inside. Mum doesn't like Skip being in the house. Skip is a smart dog. She can open the door with her paw if it is left a little bit ajar.

Mum won't let Skip in because she once did a bit of poop under the dresser. It did not smell very nice and I had to clean it up. Skip's poop reminds me a bit of . . .

'I think we can miss that bit,' says Mr Marsden who is listening to my story carefully and looking at me through the bars of the bird cage.

'Okay,' I say. 'I'll move on to the awful bit.'

4

I do not see Kim for two days because I have to visit Grandma with Mum. We leave Skip at the dog kennels all day Friday and Saturday. When we get back we collect her from the kennels. Poor Skip. She can't even put up one ear. She hates the dog kennels. She cries and whimpers whenever she has to stay there. But she is too scared of the other dogs to bark.

We drive home with Skip on my knee. She looks at me with those big brown eyes. They remind me a bit of two pools of gravy spilt on the tablecloth.

'Skip can sleep inside tonight,' I say to Mum.

'No,' says Mum. 'You tie her up in the shed, the same as always.'

Poor Skip. That night I do not tie her up. I sneak her into my bedroom and let her sleep in bed with me. She is a very clean dog. She is always licking and chewing herself.

Mum, however, has a keen sense of smell. She will know that Skip has been in. Even when you burn incense in your room Mum can still smell dog. I open the window to let in the fresh air. Then I fall asleep and have a lovely dream. All about how Kim and I and Beethoven and Skip get married and all live together on a tropical island. It reminds me a bit of one of those pretend stories that always have a lovely ending. I wish real life was like that.

The next day is Sunday. I sleep in until the sun shines on my face and wakes me up. A soft wind is blowing into the room. I get out of bed and shut the window.

Skip has gone.

5

I look out of the window and see Skip running around with a yellow tennis ball.

I think about how Mum doesn't like getting dog spit on the tennis balls. It leaves green marks on her hands.

Green marks. Our tennis balls are green.

What is that yellow thing in Skip's mouth? I jump out of the window and run down the yard. Skip sees me coming. A chase. She loves a chase. She runs off at top speed. She reminds me a bit of a rabbit bobbing up and down as it runs away from a hunter.

My heart is beating very fast. 'Please,' I say to myself. 'Let it be a ball. Let it be Mum's best glove. Let it be my new transistor radio. But don't let it be . . .' It is too awful to even say.

I run after Skip. She loves the fun. She runs under the house. 'Come out,' I yell. 'Come out, you rotten dog.' Skip does not move. 'I'll kill you,' I yell. I am shouting. There are tears in my eyes.

Skip knows that I'm mad. She rolls over on her back and begs. Way under the house where I can't even get her. She drops the yellow thing and nicks off.

Oh, no. I can't bear it. I crawl under the house on my stomach. It is dusty and dirty. There are spiders but I don't even notice them.

I stretch out my hand and I grab the little bundle of feathers. It is Beethoven. Dead. He is smeared with blood and dirt and dog spit. His eyes are white and hard. His little legs are stiff. They remind me of frozen twigs on a bare tree. Beethoven stares at me without seeing. He has sung his last song.

Tears carve tracks down my face. They run into my mouth and I taste salt.

Everything is ruined. My life is over. My dog has killed Beethoven. It is all my fault. If I had tied Skip up this would never have happened. My head swims. When Kim finds out she will cry. She will hate me. She will hate Skip.

Her mum will tell my mum. What will they do to Skip?

6

I crawl out into the back yard. Skip is wagging her tail slowly. She knows something is wrong. I feel funny inside. For a second I feel like kicking Skip hard. I feel like kicking her so hard that she will fly up over the fence.

Then I look into her gravy-pool eyes and I know that she is just a dog. 'Oh, Skip,' I cry. 'Oh, Skip, Skip, Skip. What have you done?' Then I say to myself. 'Gary, Gary, Gary, what have you done?'

I tie Skip up. Then I take Beethoven into my bedroom. He is so small and stiff and shrunken. He reminds me a bit of my own heart.

I think about Kim. She mustn't find out. What if I go and buy another yellow budgie? One that looks the same. She will never know. Kim's car is not there. They are out.

I go down to the garage and get this old golden cage that is covered in dust. When I was a little kid I used to think it was made of real gold. 'No,' Mum told me, 'it is only gilt.'

I wrap up Beethoven in a tissue and put him carefully in my pocket. Then I look in my wallet. Seven dollars. Just enough. I jump on my bike with the golden cage tied to the back. Where do they sell budgies? At the market. It is late. The market will be closing soon.

I ride like I have never ridden before. The wind whips my hair. I puff. I pant. Sweat runs into my eyes. I ride up Wheeler's Hill without getting off my bike. No one has ever ridden up Wheeler's Hill before. My heart is hurting. My legs are aching. I look at my watch. It's five o'clock. The market will be closed.

It is. The trucks are all leaving. The shoppers have gone. The ground is covered in hot-dog papers and cabbage leaves. The stalls are empty.

I look at the trucks. One or two men are still loading. I drop my bike and run from truck to truck. Car parts – no. Plants – no. Watches – no. Chocolates – no. Fairyfloss – no. I look in each truck. None have pets.

I am done. I hang my head. Beethoven is dead. Kim will hate me. Kim will hate Skip. What will happen?

I walk back slowly. Men are laughing. Children are calling. Cats are meowing.

Cats are meowing? Pets.

There is a lady with a small van and in the back are cats, dogs, guinea pigs and birds. There is a large cage full of birds.

'Please,' I yell. 'Please. Have you got any budgies?'

'They are up the back of the truck,' she says. 'I can't get them out now. Come back next week.'

'I can't,' I sob. 'I need it now.'

The lady shakes her head and starts up her van. I take Beethoven out of my pocket and unwrap him. The lady looks at the little blood-stained body. She turns off the engine with a sigh and starts to unload the van.

At last we get the cage of birds unloaded. There are canaries and finches. The cage is filled with birds. There are about twenty budgies. There are green ones and blue ones.

And there is one yellow one. It looks just like Beethoven. It is a ringer for Beethoven. I will put this bird in Kim's cage and she will never know the difference.

'Ten dollars,' says the lady. 'Yellow ones are hard to get.'

I empty my wallet. 'I only have seven dollars,' I tell her.

The lady takes my money with a smile and gently hands me the bird. 'I was young once myself,' she says.

I put the bird in my golden cage and pedal like crazy. My trip back reminds me a bit of a sailing boat skidding to shore in a storm. I hope I can get there before Kim arrives home. I have to put the new bird in the cage before she knows Beethoven is dead.

7

Finally I get home. There is no car at Kim's house yet. They are still out. I rush into the backyard and down to the aviary where the wire door is flapping in the wind. The new budgie is sitting on the perch in my golden cage. It flaps its wings.

Wings?

Beethoven only had one wing. Beethoven couldn't fly. Oh no. Kim will know straight away that the new bird is not Beethoven.

My plan has failed. I take out the little bird and stretch out its wings. It has one wing too many. 'Little bird, little bird,' I say. 'You're no good to me like this. What will I do with you?'

There is only one thing to do. I throw the tiny budgie up into the air. 'Goodbye, little bird,' I say. It flies off in a flurry of feathers and disappears for ever.

I go home.

All is lost. Kim will know what Skip has done. Kim will know what I have done. I let Skip run free.

I didn't chain her up like Mum told me. It is all my fault. I am a murderer. I am responsible for Beethoven's death.

I will never be able to look at Kim. She will never want to look at me.

Then I get an idea. I'll bury Beethoven and say nothing. Kim will think he has escaped and walked off.

No. That's no good. Kim will still think Skip opened the cage. And she'll ask me to help look for Beethoven. I would have to pretend to hunt for the bird knowing it was dead.

I get another idea. It is better. But terrible. I will sneak back to the cage and put Beethoven inside. I will lock up the cage with the brick. Kim will think that Beethoven has died of old age.

But Beethoven is covered in blood and dirt and dried-up dog spit.

I will have to clean him. I take Beethoven's body to the laundry and wash him gently. I hate myself for doing this. The blood starts to rinse out. But not all of it. I soak him for a while. I try detergent. I try soap. At last he is clean.

He is clean. And dead. And wet.

8

I go and fetch Mum's hair dryer and I dry out Beethoven's feathers until they are all fluffy and new. I gently close his staring eyes. Then, I sneak down to Kim's back yard. I remind myself a bit of a robber skulking around a jewellery shop.

I go inside the aviary door and put Beethoven down on the sawdust. No one will ever know my terrible secret. I am safe. Skip is safe. Kim will still like us. I close the door, replace the brick and go home.

That night I cannot sleep. I see Kim's sad face. I dream of myself in jail. Nobody likes me. Nobody wants me. I have caused sorrow and pain.

In the morning I look out of my window. I see Kim and her mum and dad. They are gathered around the cage. I can't hear what they are saying. I don't want to know what they are saying. Kim will be crying. Her tears will be falling. If I could see them they would remind me of a salty waterfall.

I see Kim's father put an arm around her shoulder. I wish it could be my arm. I see her mum pick up Beethoven gently in her hand.

I can't look at them any more. Everything is my

fault. Poor Skip is just a dog. I should have tied her up. Murderer. I am a murderer. And no one will ever know. My horrible secret will stay with me forever.

I get the golden cage and rush out to the garage. I cut a hole in the bottom with tin snips. I push my head through the hole. I will wear the golden cage for the rest of my life. It is my punishment. It is what I get for what I did. I will never take it off.

9

Mr Marsden is looking at me sadly. 'You made a mistake,' he says. 'A little mistake that made big things happen. But it wasn't your fault. And even if it was, you can't carry around the burden for ever. Like a rock on your shoulders. Or a cage on your head. You have to face up to it. Tell Kim. And then go on living.'

We are still sitting on the sick-room bed. Looking out of the window. A girl is slowly walking into the school grounds. She is late for school. She reminds me of a lonely ghost.

It is Kim.

Mr Marsden walks out and brings her into the

room. Her eyes are red, but still lovely. Her face is sad. It reminds me of a statue of a beautiful princess who has passed away. I cannot look at her. I shrink down in my cage.

'I'm sorry to be late,' she says to Mr Marsden. 'But something happened at home. My budgie Beethoven died on Friday. Dad says he died of old age.'

I hang my head in shame. I can't tell her the truth. I just can't.

Friday?

'Not Friday,' I say. 'Yesterday.'

'No,' says Kim. 'He died on Friday. We buried him in the back yard. But someone dug him up and put him back in the aviary.'

I take the cage off my head and throw it in the bin. After school I walk home with Kim. She holds my hand. It sort of reminds me of, well, flying free, like we are up there in the clouds with Beethoven.

Next Time Around

It all started when I was reading a comic called . . . what was it again . . .? I forget now. Anyway, this comic reckoned you could hypnotise chickens by staring them in the eye and making chook noises.

Well, it was worth a try. See, Dad had this prize chook named Rastus. It used to win ribbons at the show. He kept it in a cage in the garage and gave it nothing but the best to eat. Dad loved Rastus.

It was a smart chook. I have to admit that. You probably won't believe me when I tell you that Rastus could understand English. 'Rastus,' Dad would say. 'Count to four.' Rastus would peck on the cage four times. No kidding. It could go all the way up to twenty-two without making a mistake. It sure was brainy.

Anyway, I wanted to see if the comic was right. It would be great to hypnotise a chook. I sneaked out to the garage and let Rastus onto the floor. Then

I did what it said in the comic. I stared straight into Rastus' eyes. 'Puck, puck, puck, puck,' I said.

Rastus didn't take any notice. He just started scratching around on the ground. It didn't work. Things in comics never do. Still, I decided to give it one more try. This time I changed pitch. I made my voice higher. More like a chook's. 'Puck, puck, puck, puck,' I went.

Well, you wouldn't believe it. The silly chook froze like a statue. Its eyes went all glassy. It stood as still as a rock. Not a blink. Not a movement. It was out to it. Hypnotised. I had done it. Fantastic.

2

I walked around and around the staring chook. I poked it with my finger. It still didn't move. I grinned to myself. I could hypnotise chooks. Maybe this would make me famous. I could go on the stage. Or the TV. People would pay good money to see the boy who could put a chook into a trance.

Still and all, Dad wasn't going to like it much. He wouldn't win many ribbons with a chicken that just stood and stared.

The back door banged. I could hear Dad packing

his fishing rod in the car.

I clicked my fingers at the chook. 'Okay, Rastus,' I said. 'You can snap out of it now.'

Rastus didn't move.

I tried something different. 'When I say bananas,' I said to Rastus, 'you will wake up. You will feel happy and well. You will not remember anything that has happened.'

I took a deep breath. 'Bananas,' I said.

Rastus stared to the front like a solid, feathered soldier.

I picked him up and looked into his eyes. 'Speak to me, Rastus,' I said. 'Puck, puck, puck.' I gave him a vigorous shake.

Rastus was rigid. The rotten rooster was out like a light.

Dad's footsteps came towards the garage. 'Oh no,' I said.

I grabbed Rastus and my school bag and nicked out of the back door. Dad was going to be mad when he found out that Rastus had gone. But not as mad as he would be if he knew what I'd done. I wasn't even supposed to go anywhere near the bloomin' chook. And if I couldn't get it out of its trance it might die of starvation.

3

I made my way slowly to school with the frozen fowl tucked under my arm. Its glassy eyes stared ahead without blinking.

'What have you got there?' said a loud voice. It was Splinter, my best mate.

'It's Rastus,' I said.

Splinter whistled. 'Wow. How did he die?'

'He's not dead. He's hypnotised. I can't bring him round.'

By now we had reached the school gate. 'Pull the other one,' said Splinter.

'No, it's true,' I said. 'I'm a hypnotist. I did it.'

'Okay,' said Splinter. 'Hypnotise me then.'

I looked around the school ground. Kids were staring at me because I was standing there with a bit of petrified poultry under my arm. I could feel my face going red. 'All right,' I said. 'I will. But first I have to hide Rastus.'

We found a little trap door under one of the portable classrooms and hid Rastus inside. He looked kind of sad, staring out at us from the dark.

Splinter stretched himself out on a bench. 'Right,' he said. 'Get on with it. Put me in a trance.'

A group of kids gathered around. They were all scoffing like mad. They wanted to see me hypnotise Splinter. They didn't really think I could do it. Neither did I. A chook was one thing. But a person was another.

I took a silver pen from my pocket. 'Follow the tip of this pen with your eyes,' I said.

Splinter did as he was told. He had a big grin on his face. His eyes went from left to right like someone watching a tennis match. Suddenly the grin disappeared. Splinter's eyes went glassy. He stared to the front. Splinter was as solid as a statue.

Was he fooling? I didn't really know. I couldn't be sure. He was the sort of kid who was always playing jokes. 'You are a chook,' I said.

Splinter jumped to his feet and started crowing like a rooster. He was very good. He sounded just like the real thing; not like someone trying to copy a rooster. The kids around all gasped. They were impressed.

But I wasn't sure about it. I had a feeling that Splinter was tricking me. I had to find out. 'Splinter,' I said. 'When I count to three you will be your old self. You will not be a chook any more. But whenever you hear the word "no" you will be a chicken again for thirty seconds.'

Splinter was just opening his mouth to start crowing again. I had to be quick. 'One, two, three,' I said. Spliter shook his head and blinked. He was back to normal.

4

The school bell rang and everyone made for the doors.

'What happened?' asked Splinter. He really didn't seem to remember. I smiled to myself. I was a hypnotist. From now on nobody could give me any cheek. I would make them think they were worms. Or maggots. Life was looking good.

But not for long.

We went into the first class. Maths. With Mr Spiggot. He sure was a mean teacher. If you hadn't done your homework you had to stand up and be yelled at. Or do a Saturday morning detention. Three girls were expelled because of him. Just for giving cheek.

Mr Spiggot looked at me. 'Have you done your homework, Robertson?' he growled.

I looked at my shoes. I was in big trouble. 'No,' I answered.

'No?' he yelled.

At that very moment Splinter jumped to his feet as if someone had just switched him on. He walked around the class pecking at the floor like a chicken. 'Puck, puck puck,' he said. The class gasped. Some kids tried to smother a laugh. Splinter was in big trouble. You couldn't fool around in front of Mr Spiggot and get away with it.

Mr Spiggot started to go red in the face. I tried to figure out what was going on. And then I realised. Mr Spiggot and I had said 'no'. We put Splinter into a trance. Just like I'd told him. Splinter really did think he was a chook.

I can tell you one thing. It was the longest thirty seconds of my life. And there was nothing I could do except watch poor Splinter scratch around on the floor in front of the whole class.

Suddenly Splinter stopped. The thirty seconds was up. He looked around with a silly expression. Everyone was laughing. Except Mr Spiggot. He looked straight at me. He knew Splinter was my mate.

'Right,' he said in a very quiet voice. 'You two think you can get out of your homework by acting the fool.' He walked over to his desk and picked

53

up two sheets of paper. He gave us one each.

I groaned. It was Maths homework. Twenty hard problems.

Splinter didn't know what was going on. 'Why?' he asked, 'I haven't done anything.'

'No?' said Mr Spiggot. 'What . . .'

He didn't finish the sentence. As soon as Mr Spiggot said the word 'no', Splinter went back to thinking he was a chicken. He hopped up onto the front desk and squatted down. He put his elbows out like wings and flapped them. Then he sort of bounced up and down. He thought he was a chook laying an egg. 'Puck, puck, puck, puck,' he went.

Everyone packed up. The whole class was in fits. Mr Spiggot picked up two more sheets of sums. He held one out under Splinter's nose. Splinter pecked at his hand with his teeth. Just like a broody hen. Peck, peck, peck. 'Ouch,' shouted Mr Spiggot. He shook his hand and jumped up and down.

Splinter was still trying to lay an egg. Suddenly he stopped. The thirty seconds was up. He blinked. He stood up on the desk. Mr Spiggot was so furious that he couldn't speak. He staggered back to the desk and grabbed a handful of problem sheets. He gave us another one each.

'You two boys can leave my class,' he choked. 'And if those sums are not all finished, CORRECTLY, by tomorrow morning you will both be expelled from the school.'

5

It was no good trying to explain. He wouldn't believe me. And he might say 'no' again at any minute. We walked sadly out of the room and into the yard. We made for the portable classroom. Rastus was still there – in a trance. I put him under my arm and we started walking home. It was raining and water dripped down our backs.

'Listen,' I said to Splinter. 'I have to put you into a trance. To stop you going into your chicken act every time I say "no".'

I tried to stop myself saying the last word. 'No.' Too late. Splinter started to scratch around on the footpath. Clucking and pecking. A couple of snails were making their way across the footpath.

Splinter was hungry.

He took a snail between his teeth and hit it on the ground. Then he swallowed it in one gulp. He did the same to another and another. 'Oh, no,' I yelled.

Splinter was eating live snails. He looked around for more.

I had to do something. Quick. Before the thirty seconds were up. 'When I count to three,' I yelled. 'You will be your old self again. You will not be a chook when anyone says "no".' Then I added something else, just to be on the safe side. 'You will not remember anything about being a chook.' I took a deep breath. 'One, two, three.'

It worked straight away. Better than I thought. Splinter blinked. And winked. He rubbed his eyes. 'What happened?' he asked.

I didn't get a chance to answer him. Rastus flapped out of my arms and squawked crossly. He was his old self again. 'Rastus came out of his trance when I counted to three,' I shouted. 'It was the numbers. He understands numbers.'

Rastus looked up at me as if to agree. Then he pecked the ground three times.

Poor old Splinter wasn't interested in the chook. He waved the sheets of sums in my face. 'We have to do all of these by tomorrow,' he groaned. 'Or we're dead meat. My parents will murder me if I'm expelled from school.'

'Come round to my place after tea,' I said. 'We'll

stay up all night and work on them.'

Splinter walked home. He dragged his feet as he went. I knew how he was feeling. And it was all my fault.

6

Mum and Dad were going out that night and I had to mind the baby. 'Mum,' I said. 'Splinter and I have to do homework. I can't mind the baby.'

'Rubbish,' said Mum. 'She'll be asleep. You just want to play records. Homework? That'll be the day.' She went off laughing loudly to herself. I couldn't tell her about the sums. Or being expelled if we didn't finish them. It would be like throwing wood on a bushfire.

The baby was asleep in her bassinet. She was only eighteen months old. But boy was she fat. She'd only just started to walk. She spent all day eating.

'Here's Splinter,' said Mum. She showed him into the lounge room. 'Make sure you don't make too much noise.' She kissed me goodbye even though Splinter was there. Talk about embarrassing.

The baby snored away making sucking noises. We sat down at the table and tried to work out the answer to the first sum. It was something about water running into a bath at two litres a minute and out of the plug at half a litre a minute. You had to work out how long it would take to fill the bath.

'Strike,' said Splinter. 'How do you do it?'

'Search me,' I said. I looked at all the other sums. There were fifty altogether. Real hard ones.

'We'll never do it,' said Splinter.

My heart sank. I knew he was right. Tomorrow we would be expelled from school. We tried and tried for about an hour. But it was no good. We couldn't even work out one answer.

7

Splinter suddenly threw the papers on the floor. 'I'm sick of this,' he said. 'We might as well do something else.'

This is when Splinter had his brainwave. 'I was watching this show once,' he said. 'About a hypnotist. He could take people back in time. To earlier lives.'

'What do you mean?' I said.

He stared at me. 'Well, this bloke reckoned that everyone has lived before. Only you can't remember it. When you die, you get born again as someone else. If you were really good you might end up being born as a king or something. If you were bad in a past life you might come back as a rat.'

'I don't believe it,' I said.

Splinter was always wanting an adventure. 'Let's give it a try,' he said. 'You hypnotise me and see if I can tell you about an earlier life.'

I didn't want to do it. We were in enough trouble already. But in the end Splinter talked me into it.

'You are feeling sleepy,' I told him. Straight away Splinter started to nod off. I was getting better and better at this hypnotism lurk. 'You are going back,' I went on. 'Back to your earlier life. You are going back twenty years. It is the fifth of April at eight o'clock. Who are you?'

There was a long silence. Splinter had his eyes closed. He didn't say anything. He just sat there. It wasn't working.

Then something creepy happened. It made the hairs stand up on the top of my head. Splinter opened his mouth and spoke in a slow, deep voice. It wasn't his voice. It was the speech of a man. 'I am John Rivett,' he said.

It was amazing. I had taken him back in time. To

an earlier life. I asked him what he did for a job.

'Fireman,' he said loudly.

'How old are you?'

'Thirty-two.' He was answering my questions very seriously. I wanted to know more. This is when I made my big mistake. 'What are you doing now?' I asked. 'At this very minute?'

'Fire,' Splinter shouted. 'No time to talk. Must put out the fire.' He sat bolt upright. His eyes were wild and staring. He ran over to the sink and filled up a jug of water. Then he threw it at the wall. It ran down Mum's best wallpaper and onto the floor.

'Stop,' I yelled. But it was no good. Splinter was back in an earlier life. He thought the house was on fire. I grabbed him by the arm but he was too strong. He had the power of a grown man. He brushed me aside as if I was a baby and ran outside.

To get the hosepipe.

'When I count to three . . .' I shouted. But it was useless. He wasn't listening. He dragged the hose into the lounge and started squirting the walls. And the sofa. And the carpet. The room was soon swirling with water. I tried to grab him but he was just too strong for me.

He kept shouting something about getting the baby

out before the flames reached her. I grabbed the baby and ran into the back yard. Splinter had gone wild. He was wetting everything. He really thought the house was on fire. I had to stop him. But how? There was no one to help.

Or was there?

8

I stared down at the baby. It was sucking its knuckles and dribbling as usual. 'Baby,' I said. 'You are feeling sleepy. You are going back to another life. It is ten years ago on the third of November. Who are you? What is your name?'

The baby did nothing for a minute or so. Then it sat straight up in its bassinet. It boomed at me with this enormous deep voice. 'Lightning Larry,' said the baby. 'World Heavyweight Boxing Champion.'

'Please help me,' I said to the baby. 'Stop that maniac Splinter from flooding out the house.'

The baby jumped out of the bassinet and headed for the door. Splinter looked in amazement at the baby striding across the lawn. He didn't want an infant to get into a house that he thought was burning down. He slammed the door. The baby let fly with an enormous kick and knocked the door off its hinges.

I groaned. The house was being wrecked. The baby strode across the room to Splinter. Her nappy waggled as she walked. She drew back her arm, gave an enormous leap, and punched Splinter fair on the jaw. He dropped like a felled tree. Out to it.

The baby picked Splinter up and held him above her head. She carried him out to me and dumped him on the grass. 'How's that?' she boomed.

It was scary listening to that enormous voice coming out of such a tiny mouth. The baby gave a wicked grin and held her hands up like a boxer in a ring. 'Still the champ,' she shouted.

Splinter was starting to come round. He sat up and rubbed his jaw. 'When I count to three,' I said to both of them. 'You will forget everything that happened.'

And they did. The baby went back to being a baby and started to bawl. Splinter looked at the fractured door. 'Gee,' he said. 'You're in big trouble.'

And I was. Mum and Dad were furious when they got home. They wouldn't stop going on about it. You know the sort of thing. On and on and on. They wouldn't believe that the baby kicked the door down.

Wouldn't even let me start to explain about hypnosis. 'These lies just make it worse, lad,' said Dad.

Splinter was sent home in disgrace. I was sent to bed.

9

In the morning I woke up and hoped that it had all been a nightmare. But it hadn't. The sheets of unanswered sums were still on the floor.

When I got to school Splinter and I would be expelled. Dad and Mum would blow their tops. Life wasn't worth living.

I walked out of the door towards my doom. 'Make sure you behave yourself at school,' said Mum. I didn't answer.

I went out to check on Rastus. I stayed with him for so long that I made myself late for school.

Maths was the first class as usual. Mr Spiggot was just getting started. I rushed in right at the last minute.

'Right,' said Mr Spiggot in a low voice. 'Stand up, you two. Have you done your homework? Finished those sums?'

'No,' whispered Splinter.

'Yes we have,' I said. 'We worked on them together.'

'Okay, let's see,' said Mr Spiggot. He read out the first sum. The problem about the bath water. Then he looked at me for the answer.

'Three minutes,' I said. Mr Spiggot raised an eyebrow. I was right.

Mr Spiggot read out the next sum. It was about how many kilometres a car could travel in two days at a certain speed. 'Five hundred and two,' I said.

'Correct,' said Mr Spiggot. He read out all the sums. And I answered every one correctly. We were saved. You should have seen the look on Splinter's face.

Well, that's about all. We didn't get expelled but I was grounded for a month by Mum for all the water damage.

Looking back on it now, I would have to say that using hypnotism is not a good idea. I'm never doing it again. Never. It caused too much trouble.

If you asked me what was the worst bit, I would say it was when Splinter ate the snails. That was terrible.

And the best bit? Well, that was probably when I stopped to check on Rastus on the way to school that day. It was a great idea to send him back to an earlier life. It turned out that the silly chook had been a Maths teacher in a previous existence. I just read him the problems and he pecked out the answers. As easy as anything.

But I'll tell you what. Mr Spiggot's a Maths teacher. He'd better watch out. I reckon he'll probably be coming back as a flea next time around.

Nails

Lehman's father sat still on his cane chair. Too still.

A hot breeze ruffled his hair. He stared out of the window at the island. But he did not see. He did not move. He did not know that Lehman was alone.

But the boy knew. He realised he was trapped. Their boat had sunk in the storm. And their radio had gone with it. There was not another soul for a thousand miles. Lehman was rich. The house was his now. The whole island belonged to him. The golden beach. The high hill. The palms. And the little pier where their boat had once bobbed and rocked.

He had no more tears. He had cried them all. Every one. He wanted to rush over and hug his father back to life. He wanted to see that twisted grin again. 'Dad, Dad,' he called.

But the dead man had no reply for his son.

Lehman knew that he had to do something. He had to close his father's eyes. That was the first thing. But he couldn't bring himself to do it. What if they wouldn't move? What if they were brittle? Or cold? Or soggy?

And then what? He couldn't leave his father there. Sitting, stiff and silent in the terrible heat. He had to bury him. Where? How? He knew that no one would come. The blue sea was endless. Unbroken. Unfriendly to a boy on his own.

Lehman started to scratch nervously. His nails were growing. More of them all the time.

He decided to do nothing for a bit longer. He sat and sat and sat. And remembered how it was when they had come to the island. Just the two of them.

2

'Is that where we live?' said Lehman.

They both looked at the tumbledown hut on top of the hill. 'We'll fix it up in no time,' said Dad. 'It'll soon be like it was in the old days. When I first came here. As good as new.'

And after a while it was. It was home. Lehman became used to it. Even though he was lonely. Every morning he did his school work. Dad told him which books to read. And how to do his sums. Then he left Lehman alone with his studies. And disappeared along the beach.

Dad searched the shore. But he never let Lehman go with him. He took his camera and his knapsack. And his shovel. He peered out into the endless sea. He dug in the golden sand. And every lunch time he returned with rocks and strange objects from the sea.

'One day I'll hit the jackpot,' he said for the thousandth time. 'Maybe tomorrow. Tomorrow I'll find one. Tomorrow will be the day. You'll see.' Then he grew sad. 'There were plenty here once.' He dumped his sack in the corner. It thumped heavily on the floor.

'Let's see what you've got,' said Lehman.

Dad shook his head. 'When I find what I'm looking for, you'll be the first to know.' He picked up the sack and took it into his room. He shut the door with a smile.

Lehman knew what his father was doing. He was putting his finds into the old box. The sea chest with the heavy brass lock. Lehman longed to take a look. He wanted to know what his father was searching for. But it was a secret.

He began to scratch his fingers. Just as Dad came out of his room. 'I've told you not to do that,' said Dad.

'I'm itchy,' said Lehman. 'On the fingers. And the toes.'

'Eczema,' Dad told him. 'I used to get it when I was a boy. It'll go when the wind changes.' But he didn't look too sure. He examined the red lumps growing behind Lehman's fingernails. Then he stamped out of the hut.

3

Lehman stared around the silent bungalow. He was lonely. Dad was good company. But he was a man. Lehman wanted friends. And his mother. He picked up her photograph. A lovely, sad face. Staring at him from the oval frame. 'Where did you go?' whispered Lehman. 'I can't even remember you.'

The face seemed to say that it knew. Understood. But it was only a photo of a woman's head. A woman lost in the past. In her hair she wore a golden clip set with pearls.

During the day, Lehman kept the photo on the

kitchen table where he worked. And at night he placed it on his bedside table. It watched over him while he slept.

Lehman sighed and closed his book. He looked up as Dad came back carrying some potatoes from their vegetable patch. 'I'm going early in the morning,' he said. 'Just go on with the work I set you today. I'll be back at lunch time.'

'Let me come with you,' pleaded Lehman.

His father looked at him in silence. Then he said. 'When I find what I'm looking for. Then I'll take you.'

'It's not fair,' shouted Lehman. 'I'm all alone here. Every morning. You owe it to me to tell me what you're looking for. I don't even know what we're doing here.'

'I can't tell you,' said Dad slowly. 'Not yet. Trust me.'

That night, in bed, Lehman's eczema was worse. He scratched his itching fingers and toes until they hurt. He dreamed of dark places. And watery figures. Faces laughing. And calling. Voices seemed to whisper secrets from inside his father's sea chest.

In the morning he stared at his itching fingers. And gasped. At first he couldn't take it in. He had ten fingernails. On each hand. Another row of nails had grown behind the first ones. Clean, pink, little fingernails.

He tore back the sheets and looked at his toes. The same thing had happened. A second row of toenails had burst out of the skin. They pointed forwards. Lapping slightly over the first row.

'Dad,' he screamed. 'Dad, Dad, Dad. Look. Something's wrong with me. My nails. I've got too many nai . . .' His voice trailed off. He remembered. Dad was down at the beach. On another secret search.

4

Lehman had been told never to go down the path to the cove. Dad had told him it was dangerous. And out of bounds.

But this was an emergency. Lehman stared in horror at his hands. He pulled at one of the new nails. It hurt when he tugged. It was real. It was there to stay. He staggered as he ran down the steep track to the beach. Tears of fright and anger streamed down his cheeks. His chest hurt. His breath tore harshly at his throat.

He pounded onto the hot sand and stared along

the shore. His father was nowhere to be seen. Lehman took a guess and ran along the beach to his right. He came to a group of large rocks that blocked his way. The only way around was through the water. He waded into the gently lapping waves. The water came up to his armpits. He carefully strode on, feeling gently with his feet for rocky holes.

At the deepest point the water came up to his chin. But he was nearly round the corner now. Lehman let his feet leave the bottom. He began to swim. He rounded the rocks and splashed into a small cove that he had never seen before.

His father was digging in the pebbles against a rocky wall. At first he didn't see Lehman. Then he looked up. And noticed the dripping figure staggering out of the waves. His face broke into a radiant smile. The look of someone who has found a pot of gold. Then he saw that it was Lehman and his face grew angry.

'I told you never to come here,' he shouted. 'I can't believe that you'd spy on me. You'll ruin everything. Go back. Go back.' He wasn't just cross. He was furious.

Lehman said nothing. He just held out his hands.

Turned the backs of his fingers towards his father. There was a long silence. His father's anger melted. He stared at the double row of nails. Silently Lehman pointed to his feet. They both gazed down.

'Oh no,' said Dad. 'No. I never expected this. Not really.'

'What is it?' yelled Lehman. 'Am I going to die?'

'No. You're not going to die.'

'I need a doctor,' said Lehman.

'No,' said Dad. 'A doctor can't do anything. Not for that.'

'What is it? What's wrong with me? You have to tell me.'

They stared at each other. Both afraid.

Dad sat down on a rock. 'I can't tell you. Not yet. What I'm looking for here. It's got something to do with it. If I find what I'm looking for it will be all right. You won't have to worry. But I can't tell. Not yet.'

'What if you never find it?' said Lehman.

'I will,' said Dad. 'I have to.'

Lehman scratched the back of his hands and up his arms. The itch was growing worse. And spreading.

Dad looked around as if he was frightened of Lehman seeing something. As though he had a guilty secret. 'Go home,' he said. 'I'll pack my things and follow. We'll talk back at the house.'

5

Lehman pushed into the water. His mind swirled. His arms itched. Something was terribly wrong. He turned around and shouted back. 'What's going on? You're not telling. I've got a right to know.'

Tears pricked his eyes. Tears of anger and frustration. Dad hung his head. 'Go back,' he called. 'We'll talk. But not here.'

Lehman swam out into the swell. He passed the furthest rock and headed back to the beach on the other side. Dad was out of sight now. Lehman's feet touched the bottom and he walked through the water past a deep, black cave in the rocks.

Something moved inside.

The world froze. Lehman could hear the blood pumping in his head. A shiver spread over his skin like a wave. He choked off a cry. Two dark eyes stared out at him. He turned and thrashed through the water. Half swimming. Half running. Falling. Splashing in panic. He fell and sank under the surface. When he came up he snatched a frightened glance back at the black space between the rocks. He caught a glimpse of a man's face. Staring. Watching. Hiding.

Lehman fled along the beach, stumbling in terror, not daring to look behind him. He didn't stop until he reached the bungalow. He rushed inside. The thin walls and open windows offered no protection. But he felt better. His breath slowed. His heart beat less loudly. He looked back down the track and wondered if Dad was safe.

He scratched his elbows. And then screamed. More nails had grown. Rows and rows of them. Along his fingers and the backs of his hands. And up over his wrists.

Perfectly formed fingernails lapped over each other. They looked like two gloves of armour.

The world around began to spin. Lehman felt dizzy. His legs wobbled. He looked down. The backs of his toes, feet and ankles were covered too. A gleaming pair of toenail socks grew out of his skin. He opened his mouth to call out. And then fainted onto the floor.

6

When he awoke, the first thing Lehman saw was the photo of his mother. Her soft smile seemed to have faded. The pearl clip in her hair was dull. Then he realised that his eyes were half closed. He was staring at the world through his eyelashes. He suddenly remembered the nails. Was it a dream? He sat up and found himself on his bed. He stared at his hands. The nails had grown up his arms to his elbows. His legs were covered too. Toenails grew up to his knees.

Dad put out a hand and gently touched his shoulder. 'It's okay,' he said. 'Everything is going to be all right. Don't worry.'

Lehman smiled for a second. Dad was safe. Then he examined the nails. The smile disappeared. He was angry.

'Don't worry,' he yelled. 'Don't worry. Look at my arms. And legs. I'm covered in nails. I'm not normal. What are we doing here? What are you looking for down on the beach?' He stared at the photo next to his bed. 'What happened to my mother? I want to know what's going on.'

The wind rattled the windows and shook the bungalow. A sultry storm was brewing up. Far down below their boat tugged and pulled at the ropes that tied it to the pier.

Dad took a deep breath. 'Okay,' he said. 'It's time I told you everything.' He stood up and shut the shaking window. He raised his voice above the noise of the wind. 'I don't know where to start,' he said.

Lehman held up a nail-covered arm. 'Start here,' he cried. 'What's happening to me?' As they looked, another row of nails slowly erupted from his left arm, just above the elbow. It was like watching a flower open in fast forward. Lehman felt nothing. It wasn't painful.

Dad stroked the nails gently. As if Lehman was a cat. 'You're not sick,' he said. 'But I think more nails will grow.'

'How many more nails? Will they grow on my face? On my head? On my chest?'

Dad gave a kindly smile. 'Not your face. Maybe the rest of you though. I can't be sure. But I can find out. That's what I'm here for.'

7

There was a long silence. 'Are you looking for that man?' said Lehman.

'What man?' snapped Dad. His eyes were startled.

'I saw a face in the rocks. Down by the point. He was staring at me. Spying.'

'What did he look like?' said Dad. His voice was shrill and urgent.

'I don't know. I was scared. I only saw his eyes. I ran off.'

'This is it,' yelped Dad. 'This is what I've been waiting for. This is the answer to the problem.' He hurried off to the window and looked down at the sea. The waves were crashing now. The wind whipped at them, tearing off their foamy tops and pelting them into the humid skies.

'I'm going,' said Dad. 'Wait here. Wait here. Everything will be all right.'

'No way,' said Lehman. 'You're not leaving me behind again. I'm coming too.'

Shutters banged and a blast of wind broke into the hut like a violent burglar. Everything shook.

'There's going to be a terrible storm,' yelled Dad. 'You can't come, it's too dangerous.'

'If you go – I go,' said Lehman. He looked his father straight in the eye. They stared at each other.

'This is a once-in-a-lifetime chance,' said Dad. 'He might go. I have to . . .'

'What's it got to do with this?' yelled Lehman. He held up his arms. The nails had crept up to his shoulders. And another row was growing. Budding like an ivory chain around his neck. 'What about me? It's all right for you. Look at your skin. Normal. Look at me. Covered in nails. Don't you care?'

'It's because I care,' said Dad. He had tears in his eyes. He tried to explain. 'When we were here before. When you were young . . .'

'I don't remember,' said Lehman. 'You know I don't.'

'No,' said Dad. 'But you were here. And your mother. And that man. He might. He's our only chance to . . .'

A terrible gust of wind shook the bungalow. Thunder rumbled in the distance. The sky was torn and savage. Dad stared outside. His face was as wild as the storm. 'I have to go,' he said. 'Later. I'll explain later.' He ran to the door and vanished into the lashing wind.

8

Lehman followed his father, still dressed in nothing but shorts. He didn't feel the raging wind. Or the stinging rain. He didn't notice the nails still growing and spreading. A worse fear had filled him. He was frightened for his father. Lehman couldn't see him but he knew that he was somewhere ahead. Down the track that led to the beach.

The wind screamed and howled. Tore at his hair. Stung his eyes. He hurried on and finally found his father. He was standing at the end of the track. Staring into the furious waves which dashed up the beach and crashed into the cliff. The rocks in which the stranger had hidden were nearly covered. They were cut off by the surf. There was no safe way to get to them.

Dad peered at the sand which was revealed as the sea sucked back each wave. He measured the distance to the rocks with his eyes. Then he turned and shouted over the noise of the wind. 'Is that where he was? Is that where you saw the man?'

Lehman nodded and then grabbed his father's arm. 'Don't go,' he yelled. 'It's too rough. You won't have a chance.'

Dad snatched away his arm. He waited as a large wave began its sweep back from the beach. He jumped and ran along the sodden sand. His feet made deep, wet footprints which filled with water. The wave raced back into the sea, leaving the beach clear. A new wave ate the old and began its forward rush.

The desperate man was half way. He sank up to his ankles with each step. The wet sand slowed him to a stumbling crawl. 'Go,' whispered Lehman. 'Go, go, go.' He watched the approaching wave grow. 'Don't,' he said. 'Don't.'

The wave took no notice. It raced hungrily up the beach. It swirled around Dad's ankles. Knocked him from his feet. Buried him in its angry foam.

9

Lehman squinted and peered into the water. His father was gone. The waves were empty. Then he saw a helpless bundle washing out into the deep. Dad raised an arm. And then another. He was swimming far out. His arms flayed. He seemed to be moving into deeper water. He was helpless against the strength of the sea. 'I'm coming,' yelled Lehman. He stepped forward, waiting for the next backwash.

But before he could move, he noticed Dad riding the crest of a wave. Surfing inwards at enormous speed. A tiny, helpless cork rushing forward towards the waiting cliff.

Lehman sighed with relief. And then fright. The wave was too big. It was going to run up to the cliff and kill itself on the rocks. It seemed to gather all its strength. It flung Dad full into the jagged boulders. And then left him, hanging helplessly on a small ledge.

Without another thought, Lehman jumped onto the sand. He had to get to Dad before the next wave began its run. He made it just in time. He grabbed the stunned man by his shirt and dragged him to his feet. Dad stumbled and leaned on Lehman as the next wave crashed around them.

It sucked and pulled at their legs. Tried to topple them. But Lehman felt a strange strength. It was almost as if the sea had no power over him. He dragged his father back to the steps where they sat sodden and panting. The disappointed waves swirled and smashed below them.

Dad tried to stand. He took a few steps like a drunken man. Lehman noticed a huge swelling on his father's head. A lump as big as a tennis ball. His eyes swivelled and he started to fall.

Lehman grabbed his father by the arm. He managed to drag him, stumbling up to the house. It took all his strength. His sides ached. His chest throbbed with pain. He burst through the door and dumped his father into the chair.

Dad stared out of the window. His eyes were glazed. As the wind dropped and the storm grew still, he held out a shaking arm. He pointed down to the beach. Then he drew a deep breath, shuddered, and was still.

Lehman knew that his father was dead. Silent tears trickled down his cheeks and splashed on the nails that covered his chest. He sat there like a sorrowful knight of old. A warrior in a coat of mail. Crying for a friend who had fallen.

10

All night Lehman sat. And all morning. He'd never seen a dead person before. He didn't know what to do. Finally he stood up and walked to the door. He looked out at the sea. He wanted help. But he didn't want anyone to come.

He knew he could never leave the island. Not while he was covered in nails. He couldn't go back to the world. A world that would laugh. Or stare and wonder. He could see himself sitting in a school desk. Raising an encrusted arm.

He walked back into the room and looked at Dad. He had to do it now. Or he never would. He gently closed his father's eyes. They were soft but cold. It was like shutting a book at the end of a story. A book which would never be opened again. But a book which would never be forgotten. Not for as long as the waves beat on the lonely beach below.

Dad would be heavy. Lehman knew that. He had to dig a grave close to the house.

He chose a sandy spot that overlooked the sea. Lehman could just see the rocks jutting out where he had seen the face. He started to talk to his father as if he was still there. Standing by him.

'This is the place,' he said. 'You can see down there. Maybe what you wanted will come. Whatever it was.'

The sand was soft. He dug easily and soon had a shallow trench hollowed in the sand. It came up to his knees. He didn't want to make it too deep. Not because the work was hard. But because he couldn't bear to drop his father into a gaping hole. Something might bump. Or break.

Lehman returned to the silent man. He grabbed his father under the arms and tugged him slowly out of the door. The dead weight was heavy. Dad's feet dragged and bumped down the steps.

Lehman lowered him gently into the grave.

He looked down at the silent figure, stretched out. It was as if he was sleeping peacefully in the sand. Lehman picked up the shovel. But something was wrong. He felt bad. As if he had to do something that would hurt. Then he knew what it was. He couldn't put a shovelful of sand on his father's face. Even though he was dead.

He fetched an old newspaper from inside. Then he looked at the gentle face for the last time and covered it with the paper. He filled the hole with sand and smoothed it down. He had no strength left to make a gravestone so he pushed the shovel into the sand. And left it standing as a tall marker.

'Goodbye, Dad,' he said.

Lehman stood and stared out to sea. The sun glinted on the thousands of nails that covered almost every part of him. He looked like a tall lizard man. Standing. Waiting. Daring an invader to come.

There was no boat on the water. He didn't care. He didn't want anyone to see him as he was, covered in nails. A great feeling of loneliness filled him. As far as he knew, there was no one else in the world like him.

11

He walked inside and looked in the mirror. His face was clear. But his chest, back, arms and legs were covered in the new nails. He suddenly opened a drawer. And pulled out some nail clippers. He wondered if he would have to spend his life clipping thousands of nails as they grew. He laughed wildly and threw the clippers out of the open window.

It had taken him all afternoon to dig the grave.

The sun was beginning to sink lower in the sky. In an hour or two it would be dark. And he was alone. He wondered if he should lock the windows. And bolt the door. He knew that tonight – when the dark came – he would be frightened.

The face in the cave would come. Creeping. Stealing up the path. Wandering in the shadows. He knew that he would jump at every sound. He would try not to sleep. But in the end sleep would come. And so would the unknown man.

He jumped to his feet. 'You won't get me,' he shouted. 'I'll get you.'

He ran outside and sharpened a long stick with the axe. Now he had a spear. He marched down the path towards the beach. His legs felt weak. His stomach was cold and heavy. He wanted to turn. And run. And hide.

But he forced himself on until he reached the beach. The sea was still and blue. It lapped gently on the sandy beach. The wild waves had gone. Lehman strode along the sand towards the rocks. And the cave.

He shuddered even though the air was warm. He gripped the spear tightly with his nailed fingers. The tide was out and the small cave now opened onto the sand. He reached the entrance and peered into the gloom.

There were soft, dripping noises. And the sound of steady breathing. Someone was in there.

'Come out,' he shrieked. His voice cracked and ended in a squeak. He coughed and tried again. 'Come out, whoever you are.' The words echoed in the cave. Then something moved. He thought he heard a slippery, rustling noise.

His courage fled. He started walking backwards, too frightened to turn around.

12

Three people came out of the cave. If people is the word. Two men. And a smaller one. They wore no clothes. But instead, were covered from neck to toe – in nails.

Lehman felt faint. He couldn't take it in. He wondered if this island gave people the terrible nail disease.

They smiled at him. Warm, friendly smiles. The child giggled nervously. The nail people were wet. They had been in the sea. Water glistened and sparkled from their nails. They shone like neat rows of wet glass.

One of the men pointed into the deep water further out. A swift shadow like a shark circling moved far down. It rushed towards the shore with the speed of a train. Then burst out of the water and back in again.

Lehman caught a glimpse of a sparkling fish tail. And fair hair. It swirled several times. And then climbed onto a rock. A woman with long golden hair. And a fish tail covered in nails.

The men laughed. Their chuckles sounded like bubbles bursting out of the water. Lehman stared at the nails which shivered as they moved. He spoke aloud. Half to himself. Half to them. 'Not nails,' he said, 'but scales.'

He turned back to the mermaid. In her hair, she wore a golden clip, set with pearls. The same pin that he had seen every day in his mother's photograph.

In that moment Lehman knew that while his father had been a man, his mother was a mermaid.

She beckoned to him, calling him out into the water. Then she dived down under the rippling surface. The mermen nodded at him, pointing out to sea. Like Lehman, they had legs rather than a tail.

Lehman walked. And walked. And walked. The waves closed over his head. He opened his mouth and took a deep breath of water. It passed through his new gills with a fizz of bubbles. His head was filled with lightness. And happiness. He began to swim, deep down, following his mother.

Then, for a second, he remembered something. He burst upwards faster and faster and plunged out of the water like a dolphin. He snatched one last look at the island. And saw, high on a hill, a small mound. A shovel stood pointing to the bright sky above. He knew now why his father had brought him here. A fish-boy could only be happy in one place – the ocean.

Lehman waved goodbye and then plunged down far below the surface. And followed his family out to sea.

Yuggles

See, no one had ever seen a yuggle before. And no one's ever seen one since. Where they came from and how they exploded has never been explained. Anyway, I'm getting a bit ahead of myself. I'd better start at the beginning.

This boy called Pockets was visiting his little sister Midge in hospital. Pockets called in every day to try and cheer her up. The poor little kid – she was really sick. Mostly she just lay with her head on the pillow looking at you sadly with those big brown eyes. It was pretty hard getting a smile out of her.

'The prize is an Easter egg,' said Pockets. 'The biggest bloomin' Easter egg in the world.' He stretched out his hands like a fisherman telling lies about his catch. 'It's covered in little chocolate angels,' he went on. 'Hundreds of 'em.'

Something unusual happened when Pockets said

this. Midge smiled. Only a little smile, filled with pain. But a smile all the same. 'I'd sure like to see that egg,' whispered Midge. 'I'd love to see those angels.'

Well, this was enough for Pockets. 'If you want that egg, Midge,' he said, 'me and Cactus will get it for you.'

Pockets' mate Cactus stood at the end of the bed. He smiled back at Midge. But inside he wasn't smiling. He was wondering how they were going to keep Pockets' promise.

2

'How are we going to win that egg?' said Cactus as they walked home from the hospital. 'Now you've gone and got her hopes up. What if we don't come first? There's only one prize.'

'We'll win,' said Pockets. 'All we have to do is collect more mushrooms than anyone else.'

'Everyone else wants to win too,' said Cactus. 'The whole school is after that Easter egg. Everyone'll be searching.'

'No one wants to win more than us,' said Pockets. 'We'll search all day. And we'll search all night. That way we're sure to find the most.'

'All night,' yelled Cactus. 'My dad won't let me out at night. Nor will yours.'

'What they don't know won't hurt 'em,' said Pockets. He was like that, was Pockets. Didn't care what happened if it was something for poor little Midge.

Well, Pockets and Cactus searched all day for mushrooms. And they found plenty. They trudged through the paddocks in the pouring rain. They walked and walked until their feet grew blisters as big as eggs. Their bag of mushrooms was so heavy they could hardly carry it.

But they kept going. On and on. Bending. Picking. Searching. Running over to each new clump of mushrooms as if it might vanish before they got there.

Just before tea, they saw something bad. In the next paddock. It was Smatter, the school bully. He and his mate Johnson were looking for mushrooms too. And they carried a large sack of mushrooms.

'Oh no,' said Pockets. 'Look at that sack. They've nearly got as many as us.'

3

That's how it was that Pockets and Cactus came to be out in the paddocks at night. In the dripping rain. It was their only chance to make sure they found more mushrooms than Smatter and Johnson. In the feeble light of their torches they stumbled through the grass. Every now and then finding a sodden but precious mushroom.

The sack grew heavier and heavier. 'Let's leave it here for a while,' said Pockets. 'We can come back and get it later.' He dumped the precious sack down under a dark tree. The two boys set off carrying only a small bucket. They didn't notice another torch flashing between the bushes. Nor did they know that more than mushrooms were growing in the cold, wet night.

Luck was against them. Cactus and Pockets searched and stumbled through the wet grass. But they found nothing. Not a single mushroom. Not so much as the smell of one.

'It's okay,' said Pockets wearily. 'We've got enough already. Smatter can never get as many as us now. I can't wait to see the look in Midge's eyes when she sees that Easter egg. Let's get the sack and go home.'

With squelching feet they made their way back to the tree. 'Where's the sack?' grumbled Cactus. His dying torch beam searched the wet grass. The sack wasn't there.

'Is this the right tree?' said Pockets. His voice shook as he spoke.

Cactus shone the torch up into the branches. 'There it is,' he yelled. 'Someone's thrown it up into the tree. Give me a bunk up.' Cactus scrambled up the wet gum tree. Dripping leaves mopped his face. Water trickled down his back. Suddenly Cactus slipped. He slithered down, scraping the skin off his knee. He swung for a moment from a bucking branch. Then, slowly, painfully, he hooked one leg over the branch and dragged himself up. He climbed carefully to where the sack dangled from a fork in the branches.

Cactus just managed to hook the sack with one finger and pull it towards him. It came away easily. Lightly. He peered into the sack and gasped. There was only one little mushroom in the sack. Otherwise, it was empty. 'They're gone,' he shouted down through the branches.

'Someone's nicked 'em,' yelled Pockets. Rage choked his words. They had worked all day. And all night. For nothing. Now Midge would never get the giant chocolate Easter egg. The thought of his little sister lying in hospital was too much for Pockets. He punched the tree with his fist and skinned his knuckles. Blood ran down his fingers. He wiped his eyes with a knuckle. It made the tears on his cheek turn red.

Far off, along a ridge of darkness, two torches twinkled between the trees. 'After 'em,' yelled Cactus. 'We can catch 'em at the road.'

4

The two friends charged into the night. They plunged across a small creek and headed up the hill to the road. Just in time. Two large figures loomed out of the shadows. They carried an enormous sack. Pockets and Cactus could smell freshly picked mushrooms.

'Drop those mushrooms,' yelled Pockets. 'You pinched 'em out of our sack.'

Smatter and his off-sider stopped and peered at their enemies. They were the biggest kids in the school. They were tough. Real tough. 'Prove it,' said Smatter. 'These are ours. We picked every one ourselves.' He bunched up his fist.

Pockets wanted to fight them. He felt anger

growling in his throat. But he knew it was useless. They were just too big. There was no way he and Cactus could beat the bullies.

Smatter knew that he'd won. He laughed cruelly. 'Wimps,' he chortled as he headed off into the night.

By now the rain had stopped and the sun was rising over the bush. A kookaburra laughed. But Pockets and Cactus didn't join in.

'It's hopeless,' said Cactus. 'Even if we could find more mushrooms it's too late. The competition ends at ten o'clock. There's not enough time left.'

Pockets didn't answer. He was thinking about little Midge. Poor kid. She'd been in hospital most of her life. If you could call it a life. She hardly ever asked for anything. And now he couldn't even get the one thing she did want. It wasn't as if he could go off and buy another one. This was the best chocolate Easter egg ever made. And anyway he didn't have any money.

Pockets stared at the ground. Cactus made a despairing search for mushrooms. 'Give up,' said Pockets. 'It's too late.'

Cactus didn't reply. He was peering at something on the ground 'Look at this,' he yelled 'Whopping big mushrooms.'

'They're brown,' said Pockets. 'They're no good. They're toadstools. Probably poisonous. Don't touch 'em.'

'I'm taking 'em anyway,' said Cactus. 'They might be valuable.' He dropped the three toadstools into the sack. 'Wonder what they're called?' he said.

'Yuggles,' said Pockets.

Pockets was always making up names for things. It was just a strange habit he had.

'Okay,' said Cactus. 'Yuggles it is.'

'It's getting light,' said Pockets. 'We'd better get home before our parents wake up. I'll meet you at eight-thirty at my place.' They ran off in different directions. Pockets took the sack with him. Inside, the yuggles jiggled, quietly. They didn't make a sound.

5

Pockets sneaked home to bed. After a bit he got up and had breakfast. Then he met Cactus at the gate and they walked to school together. 'What did you bring them for?' said Cactus pointing to the sack.

Pockets took out one of the brown toadstools. He gave it a sniff. 'It smells awful,' he said. 'Yuck.'

They stopped outside a shop. It was Took's Real

Estate agency. On the window someone had sprayed brown graffiti. It said TOOK IS A ROOKER.

Suddenly the door of the shop burst open. Mr Took rushed out and grabbed Pockets by the scruff of the neck. 'Got you,' he screamed. 'You little devil. I'll teach you to write on my window.'

'I didn't,' babbled Pockets.

'Don't give me that,' yelled Took. His eyes bugged out in his head like jelly marbles. 'Look at your fingers, they're covered in brown paint.'

Pockets stared at his hands. They were brown. 'It's the toadstool,' he said, holding it up in front of Took's face. 'It's not paint. It's toadstool.'

Took was furious. He smacked the toadstool out of Pockets' hand. It bounced across the footpath and stopped near a dustbin.

'It's true,' said Cactus. He walked towards the yuggle. Then he stopped. Something was happening. The toadstool moved. It wobbled. Then it began to change shape. It grew and lost its toadstool shape. It turned into a large brown blob like a lump of clay.

And then, just as if it was being formed by invisible hands, it changed into a rubbish bin. It turned into a bin. Exactly the same as the one on the footpath. It even had the same broken handle and large dent on the top. Twin bins, standing silently together.

Mr Took screamed. He rubbed his eyes. He blubbered and blabbered. 'What? How? Quick, help, run. No, no, no.' He seemed to want to run. But like Pockets and Cactus he couldn't tear himself away.

The next bit is hard to believe. But it really happened. The new bin seemed to have a problem. It is hard to explain. It was sort of like it was holding its breath. As if it was going to explode with the effort of staying together. Nothing happened for about two or three minutes. The bin just kind of stood there. Perhaps it gave a wobble. But mostly it just put all its effort into staying a bin.

6

Mr Took took a step forward. Carefully, mind you. Not in a brave way. But like someone who sees a hundred dollar note in a snake's mouth. He just had to get a bit closer.

Then it happened. The new bin gave three little squeaks. And erupted. Like a volcano. It bubbled and burst into a horrible brown sludge. A mountain of muck. It was putrid. Mr Took screamed and fell back onto the footpath.

Cactus and Pockets stared in horror.

'Aaaagh,' bellowed Pockets.

'Uugh . . .' yelled Cactus.

The revolting brown goo blistered and plopped like a hot mud pool. 'Disgusting,' gasped Cactus. 'It looks like brown vomit.'

'Foul,' said Pockets.

Mr Took crawled back into his shop and locked the door. The two boys were alone with the pile of rotting brown gunk.

'What is it?' groaned Cactus. He stared at the horrible lumps that festered and swam in the remains of the melted bin.

Pocket scratched his head. 'It's brommit,' he said. 'We'll call it brommit.'

Mr Took burst out of his door carrying a broom and a shovel. He stared nervously at the brommit. He didn't want to get too close. He shouted angrily. 'You two can clean that stuff . . .'

He never finished the sentence. Pockets and Cactus were already running down the street as fast as they could go. The sack with the mushroom and the last two yuggles in the bottom bumped against Pockets' knee.

Finally they stopped on a corner. They puffed and

panted. Cactus had a pain in his side. Pockets stared nervously behind him. 'There's no one there,' he gasped. 'We're safe.'

7

'I can't believe what happened,' said Cactus. 'That yuggle turned into a bin.'

'Then it squeaked three times,' said Pockets.

'And melted into brown vomit,' added Cactus.

'You mean brommit,' said Pockets.

They grinned at each other. But not for long.

'Get them,' screeched a voice. 'Get 'em, boy.'

A fierce growl made them turn. An enormous dog snarled and salivated. It snapped at their ankles with teeth like steel. Its red eyes bulged with hate. It darted in and out, looking for a chance to tear and rip at their unprotected legs.

'Go, boy. Get 'em, get 'em,' shouted a woman from behind a hedge. Pockets looked at the woman. Her eyes were as fierce and angry as the dog's. 'I've told you not to stand on my grass,' she shrieked. 'Go, Bandit, go.'

Pockets and Cactus wanted to turn and run. But they were too scared. 'Keep your eyes on him,' whispered Cactus. 'Don't move.'

The dog's growl grew even more terrible. It pulled back its lips like a curtain to reveal green and jagged teeth. It circled, waiting for its chance.

Pockets looked for a weapon. A stick. A stone. Anything. But the grass was bare. Without really knowing why, he put his hand in the sack and pulled out a yuggle.

He felt a tingle in his fingers. A small vibration. A sort of frightened quiver. He threw the yuggle at Bandit. It hit the dog on the head and dropped onto the nature strip. The dog renewed its attack. Barking and lunging forward.

Then it stopped. And sniffed.

The yuggle had begun to grow. It bubbled and fizzed like brown soapsuds pouring out of a washing machine. Then it began to take shape. A bulge formed at one end. Four muddy stick legs grew underneath it. It sprouted fur.

The yuggle turned into a dog. A frozen copy of the savage animal that snapped and snarled around it. Not a live dog. More like a stuffed dog. A replica of Bandit. It had fur. It had red swollen eyes. And its mouth was pulled back in a solid snarl. But it wasn't alive. It was only a statue. Of sorts.

Bandit growled and circled the new dog. It sniffed and snuffed. The woman peered over the fence in terrified silence. Pockets gave a nervous smile and stepped back. Cactus followed him. Time seemed to stand still. The minutes ticked by. Nothing moved except Bandit who darted in and out, snapping at its silent twin.

The yuggle dog quivered, just for a second. It gave a tense little shiver. Then it squeaked three times.

'Oh no,' yelled Pockets. 'It's going to collapse.' He moved back. Bandit moved closer.

The copy of Bandit couldn't keep it up. A bulge like a boil grew on its head. It suddenly erupted and a brown river of brommit poured out. Bandit grabbed the decaying dog in its teeth. The yuggle dog burst and melted into a brown stinking mess on the grass.

Bandit's nose was covered it in. The poor animal yelped and wiped at its snout. It rolled over on the grass, rubbing its mouth on the ground in a pitiful effort to remove the smell. Then it gave a yelp and a squeal. And raced down the street at enormous speed. The woman took one last horrified look at the brommit. Then she ran after her dog. 'Bandit,' she called. 'Bandit, come back.'

8

Pockets and Cactus ran too. They didn't stop until they reached the school gate. They didn't even notice the kids milling around the gym waiting for the mushroom weigh-in.

'Boy,' said Pockets. 'These yuggles are dangerous.'

'Maybe we should get rid of it,' said Cactus slowly.

Pockets peered into the bag at the last yuggle and the one lonely mushroom next to it. 'Nah,' he said. 'It might be useful. We can still win that Easter egg, you know. If we use our brains.'

'How?' asked Cactus.

'This yuggle might be able to help,' said Pockets. He reached into the bag and pulled out the last yuggle. He held it up and stared at it. Then he reached down and took out the little mushroom. 'Go on,' he said to the yuggle. 'Change.' He rubbed the yuggle and the mushroom together. Nothing happened.

'Something's missing,' said Cactus slowly. 'It's not going to change. You know what? I think it only changes when someone mean is around. Maybe when it's scared. Mr Took was real mean. And so was that woman with the dog. The yuggle only changes if someone nasty is around.'

Pockets was desperate. He thought of poor little Midge in hospital. He thought of that enormous Easter egg covered in chocolate angels. He thought of the bag of mushrooms that had been stolen. The prize should have been his. He watched sadly as kids walked into the gym carrying bags of mushrooms. None had a bag as big as the one that had been stolen. None except Smatter, that is.

9

Smatter and Johnson staggered up to the door carrying an enormous sack between them. They sneered at Pockets and his little mushroom and toadstool. Then they disappeared inside.

'That's it,' yelled Pockets. 'I can't take any more of this.' He was trying not to cry.

'What are you going to do?' asked Cactus in a worried voice.

'I'm going in,' said Pockets. 'With the last yuggle. If it won't do its thing, well I'll . . .'

'You'll what?' said Cactus.

'I'll nick the Easter egg.'

'Steal it?' yelled Cactus.

'Yeah,' answered Pockets. 'It's in a fridge, out the back. I'll take it and escape out the back door. Everyone will be too busy watching the weigh-in. No one will know.'

'You can't,' said Cactus. 'It would be stealing.'

'No it won't,' yelled Pockets. 'It should be mine. We had the most mushrooms. Smatter stole them.'

Without another word Pockets rushed into the hall.

'I'm not coming,' shouted Cactus. 'Not if you're going to steal it.' Cactus stood there, looking at the gym and listening to the shouts and cheers coming from inside. He felt sorry for Midge. But stealing the egg wasn't the answer.

Minutes ticked by. Half an hour passed. Cactus waited and worried. Suddenly an enormous cheer went up inside the hall. Cactus wondered what had happened. It didn't take long to find out.

Smatter had won the competition. He burst out of the door followed by dozens of cheering kids. He held the enormous Easter egg above his head like a trophy. Then he spotted Cactus standing there looking at his boots. Smatter smirked. 'Suffer,' he yelled at Cactus.

Cactus felt the anger boiling inside him. But he didn't say anything. Not a word. Smatter came over. He broke a chocolate angel off the egg and ate it. He stuffed it into his mouth. Then he started eating the egg. In front of everybody.

'Pig,' said Cactus.

'You think I'm a pig,' said Smatter. 'Just watch this then.' He broke off enormous chunks of chocolate and stuffed them into his mouth. No one had ever eaten so fast. Or so greedily.

Cactus felt his heart sink inside him. He thought of grabbing the remains of the egg and running for it. But it wouldn't be any good now. Little Midge wouldn't want a half-eaten egg. And anyway all the chocolate angels had already disappeared down Smatter's gullet.

Cactus took a step forward. He couldn't control himself. He wanted to punch Smatter on the nose. But before he could move, he noticed something. It was Pockets. He was waving through the gym window. Making signals. And shaking his head. Cactus stopped. And watched as Smatter scoffed down the whole Easter egg. What a guts. No one else even got a taste.

10

Smatter looked around at the crowd of kids outside the gym. They couldn't believe that anyone could scoff so much chocolate in so short a time.

Just as Smatter was wiping the last traces from his lips, Pockets burst out of the door. He was carrying another Easter egg. It was exactly the same as the one Smatter had just eaten. Even the little angels were identical.

Cactus couldn't take it in. He tried to work out what was going on. The yuggle must have copied itself into an Easter egg. And Pockets was carrying it. 'Drop it,' screamed Cactus. 'Run for it.'

Pockets just smiled. He wasn't scared at all.

Smatter stared at the egg in Pockets's hands. His mouth fell open. But he didn't say anything. Not a word. He just stood there sort of quivering. And then something strange happened. He gave three little squeaks. Or, to be more exact, three little squeaks came out of his mouth.

Cactus stared at Pockets. He pointed at Smatter with a question on his face. Pockets nodded. 'He's eaten the yuggle,' he yelled.

Well, it was horrible. Just horrible. You wouldn't

want me to tell you how that brommit came pouring out of Smatter's mouth. You really wouldn't want to know how everyone screamed and jumped back from the foul flow. It was too terrible to tell. Too terrible.

But you probably won't be surprised to hear that Smatter didn't want the real Easter egg. Neither did anyone else. Except Pockets.

It was something to see when he took it to the hospital. Little Midge's face lit up. She had the biggest smile. She just couldn't believe it when Pockets walked in the door with that egg all covered in chocolate angels.

Grandad's Gifts

'We can't open that cupboard,' said Dad. 'I promised my father. Grandad locked it up many years ago and it's never been opened.'

'What's in it?' I asked.

'No one knows,' said Mum.

'But it's in my bedroom,' I said. 'I need to know what's in it. It could be anything.'

'I lived in this bedroom for nineteen years,' said Dad. 'And I kept my promise. That cupboard has never been opened. Now I want you to promise me that you'll never open it.'

They both looked at me, waiting for my answer. Suddenly there was a knock on the door downstairs. 'It's the removal van,' said Mum. 'About time too.'

Mum and Dad rushed down to help move in our furniture. I wandered around my new room. It was small and dusty with a little dormer window over-looking the tangled garden.

No one had lived in the house for years. It was high in the mountains, far from the city. The garden was overgrown. Ivy had climbed the gum trees. Blackberry bushes choked the paths and strangled the shrubs.

I walked over to the forbidden cupboard and gave the handle a shake. It was locked firm. I put my eye to the keyhole but everything was black. I sniffed under the gap at the bottom of the door. It was musty and dusty. Something silent inside seemed to call me.

It was almost as if a gentle voice was stirring the shadows of years gone by. The stillness seemed to echo my name, 'Shane, Shane, Shane . . .'

2

'Shane.' Mum shouted up the stairs. 'Come and help bring these things in.'

They were lifting a large machine from the van. The removalist man had one corner and there was one left for me. 'Quick, grab it,' said Dad. 'It's heavy.'

I helped lower the machine onto the ground. 'What is it?' I asked.

'A mulcher,' Dad told me. 'You put in branches and leaves and twigs and it chews them up into mulch. We're going to use it to clear up this garden.'

I stared around at the tangled yard. That's when I saw the two lemon trees for the first time. A big one over near the gate. And a small, shrivelled up one near the back fence. The big tree was covered in lemons. But the small one had only two. It wasn't much of a tree.

Dad pointed to the big lemon tree. 'It's always grown well,' he said. 'Grandad shot a fox. He buried its remains under that tree.'

I gave a shiver. I knew that I would never peel one of those lemons. Or eat one.

I carried a box back to my room and started to unpack. I turned my back on the secret cupboard and tried not to listen to the gentle voice lapping like waves in my head. 'Shane, Shane, Shane . . .'

Once again I peered through the keyhole. This time I thought I saw two points of light twinkle in the darkness. I shivered. This was creepy. I didn't really want to live in this room.

3

That night I couldn't sleep. Every time I opened my eyes I saw the cupboard door. After a long time I finally drifted off. I had a wonderful dream about trees. The branches reached out and stroked me. They lifted me high into the air and passed me along the roof of the forest. I was filled with a wonderful floating power. The soft branches took me wherever I wanted to go.

In the morning I woke feeling wonderful. Instead of getting dressed I decided to move the bed. I wanted to sleep so that I could see out of the window. The bed was old and heavy. It wouldn't move. I could see that it had been in that spot for years and years.

I ran outside and fetched a long plank. I used it to lever the bed. After a lot of creaking it started to move. Inch by inch. Finally I had it up against the window. The place where the bed had been was covered in dust. I swept it up gently.

The floor creaked under my feet. I knelt down and looked. There was a loose board.

'Breakfast,' yelled out Mum.

'Coming,' I shouted back.

I tried to prise up the board but it wouldn't budge.

Suddenly it gave way and sprang out. It was almost as if a hidden hand had heaved it up.

I stared inside. Something glinted dully. I reached down and pulled out a rusty key.

'Shane,' yelled Mum.

'Coming,' I called. I shoved the key in my pocket and raced downstairs. I bolted my breakfast down. I was sure that the key would fit the door of the cupboard. The cupboard I had been forbidden to open.

'You can help me today,' said Dad. 'I'm going to cut back the overgrown trees and put the branches through the mulcher.'

I groaned inside. I was dying to run up and try the key in the cupboard. Now I wouldn't get a chance until after tea. Dad was a slave driver. He'd give me a big lecture about laziness if I tried to nick off.

4

All day we worked; cutting down branches and feeding them into the mulcher. It roared and spat out a waterfall of woodchips. It was amazing how it could turn a whole tree into sawdust in no time at all.

'Are you going to cut down the lemon trees?' I asked.

'Yes,' said Dad. 'I'm putting in native plants. Go on, you can go now. Thanks for helping.'

I ran up to my room and shut the door. Then I took out the rusty key and walked over to the cupboard. I put it in the lock and tried to move it. Blast. It didn't seem to fit. I jiggled and wiggled it. Then, just like the floorboard, it moved without warning. As if hidden fingers had twisted it.

The doorknob turned easily. I swung open the door.

The fox didn't move. It had been dead a long time. It hung from a hook at the back of the cupboard. Its body was flat as if it had been run over by a steam roller. Its long, bushy tail hung almost to the floor. Its eyes stared ahead without movement. They were made of glass. I could see that they were sewn on like buttons.

Suddenly the fox moved. Its mouth opened a fraction. My brain froze. The world seemed to spin. I was filled with terror. I gave a scream and slammed the door shut. Then I ran downstairs.

Tea was on the table. I didn't know what to do. Had the fox's mouth really opened? It couldn't have.

Maybe I had disturbed it with the breeze of the door opening.

I wanted to tell Dad and Mum. But they had ordered me not to open the cupboard. Dad had lived in that room for all those years and he had never opened it. I could just hear him giving me a lecture. 'One night,' he would say. 'You couldn't even go one night without breaking your word.'

I hadn't given my word actually. But that wouldn't make any difference. An order is an order.

As I ate my tea I thought about the fox. I'd seen it somewhere before. Then suddenly I realised. On the kitchen wall was an old photo of Grandad. Behind him was a hall stand. There were hats and scarves and umbrellas hanging on it. And a fox skin.

'What's that thing?' I said to Dad. I jumped up and pointed to the fox skin.

'A fox fur. It's the one Grandad shot. He preserved the skin and made it into a fur wrap for Grandma. But she wouldn't wear it.'

'Why not?'

'She said that she wasn't going to wear a dead animal around her neck. She felt sorry for it. She said it looked as if it was alive. Grandad was disappointed that she didn't like his gift.'

'What happened to it?' I asked.

'No one knows,' said Dad. 'I couldn't find it after Grandad died.'

'It might be in that locked cupboard,' I said.

Dad looked at me in a funny way. I went red. 'If it is,' he said, 'it stays there. A promise is a promise.'

We all looked at the picture. 'Pity the photo's only brown,' said Dad. 'That coat of Grandad's was bright red. And his eyes were the clearest blue.'

I wasn't really interested in the colours that weren't in the photo. I was in a real pickle and I didn't know what to do. I had to sleep in a room with a dead fox in the cupboard. Why had Grandad locked the door and made everyone promise not to open it? What was it about that fox?

5

That night I dreamed more dreams about trees. But this time it was lemon trees. Or should I say lemon tree. A voice seemed to call me. It wanted me to go to the large lemon tree. The voice inside my head told me to go out into the night. And pick a lemon.

I cried out and sat up in bed. The cupboard door had swung open. The fox's glass eyes glinted in the moonlight. I thought it moved. It seemed to sigh gently.

Suddenly I knew I had nothing to fear. The fox was my friend. It was sad. Lonely. Lost.

I walked over and gently reached out. I stroked the soft fur with my hand. Dust fell softly away. A great sadness swept over me. The fox was like a beautiful empty bag. Its bones and heart and life were long gone.

And I knew where they were.

'All right,' I said. 'I'll do it.'

The fox made no answer. It hung limply like the moon's cast-off coat. I crept down the stairs. Mum and Dad were asleep. I walked between the shadows until I reached the large lemon tree. Where the carcass of the fox had been buried, many years before.

The ripe lemons drooped between the silvery leaves. I knew which one to pick. My hand seemed to have a life of its own. It reached up and plucked a lemon from high on the tree.

I tiptoed back inside the house and crept up the silent stairs. The cupboard was open like a waiting mouth. I wasn't sure what to do with the lemon. The fox skin hung silently on its peg. I gently opened its jaws and placed the lemon between its teeth. Then I shut the door and jumped into bed.

I pulled the pillow over my head. But even so, I could hear a gentle chewing, sucking, swallowing sound from behind the door.

The fox was feasting.

I finally fell asleep. Deep in carefree slumber.

6

In the morning I peered into the cupboard. At first I thought that nothing had changed. The fox fur still flopped from its peg. But the lemon had gone. I stroked the fox. I ran its tail between my thumb and finger. At the very tip of its tail I stopped. It was hard inside, as if a piece of a broken pencil had been inserted there. It was a small bone.

I gasped. That bone had not been there the day before.

The next night I visited the lemon tree again. Again I fed the fox. And again his tail grew firmer. Strengthened by another bone.

Each day I helped my father chop the trees and feed the mulcher. And each night I fed the fox from the lemon tree.

At the end of two weeks the fox was round and plump. Its fur had lost its dust. It glistened, strong and full. It was a fine fox. But it still hung from the peg. Its head flopping near the floor.

My work was nearly done. On the second-last night I placed my hand on its chest.

I can't describe the thrill that ran up my arm. The fox's heart was beating. It was alive but not alive. It still dangled from the peg. But its nose was wet and warm. A red tongue trembled between its teeth.

I had done my work. The lemons had given back what my grandfather had taken and buried beneath the tree. I opened the cupboard door wide. 'Go,' I said. 'This is your chance.'

The fox didn't answer. Didn't move. Something was wrong.

The glass eyes stared without life.

The eyes. It needed its real eyes.

7

I stared out of the window at the first signs of the day. The last two lemons glowed redly in the sunrise. The tree stretched upwards from its roots. Its branches were like arms offering gifts from below.

'Tomorrow,' I said. 'Tomorrow I'll get your eyes.'

I closed the door and snuggled down into my bed. I fell asleep for many hours.

The sound of the mulcher drilled away at my slumber. There was something wrong. In my dreams I knew it. I sat upright and listened to Dad feeding branches into the hungry machine.

'No,' I yelled. 'No.' I ran to the window. 'Stop,' I screamed. 'Stop.'

I was too late. The lemon tree was nothing but a pile of wood chips. I ran down the stairs in my pyjamas and bare feet. 'The lemons,' I shouted. 'Did you save the last two lemons?'

Dad looked up in surprise. 'No,' he said. 'They were green.'

Tears ran down my face. I thought of the blind fox, still hanging in the blackness of the cupboard that for so long had been its coffin. I stood there and sobbed.

'They're only lemons,' said Dad. 'For goodness' sake. What a fuss.'

I couldn't tell him. I couldn't say anything. I trudged back to my room. 'I'm sorry, fox,' I said. 'Now you'll never see.'

A voice floated in the window. It was Dad. 'This

little lemon tree still has two lemons, Shane. If you want lemons, why don't you take these?'

I stared sadly down. That tree wasn't any good. It wasn't growing where the fox had been buried. Still and all, it was worth a try.

8

I waited all day. I waited until the sun had set and the moon filled the evening. I walked slowly. Not really hoping. But wanting so badly to give the fox my last gifts.

The lemons seemed to tremble. They dropped into my hands as I reached up. As though they had been waiting.

What was inside? For a moment I wondered what I would see if I peeled the lemons. Two eyes? Or just pith and pips and lemon pulp? I shuddered.

I placed the lemons between the white teeth of my friend the fox. And shut the door. I heard nothing. No sighs. No chomps. No swallows.

I had failed the fox.

Slowly I walked downstairs to supper. Dad and Mum tried to cheer me up. 'Are you ill?' said Mum.

'Yes,' I said. 'I think I am. But you can't fix it with medicine.'

Dad looked up. 'What was that?' he said. 'I thought I heard something upstairs. Someone's in the house.'

We all ran up to my room. The cupboard door was open. The window was open. Dad looked at the empty cupboard. And then at me. I nodded my head. I didn't care what he said or what he did. I was happy in a way that I had never been happy before. I picked up the two glass eyes that lay rejected on the floor.

'Look,' shouted Mum.

On the edge of the garden, under the little lemon tree, stood a magnificent fox. Its tail glistened in the silver light. Its shoulders shivered. Its ears pricked and pointed towards us. It took our scent and turned and gazed.

We all gasped. 'Look at its eyes,' whispered Mum.

The fox stared at us. Unafraid. Its large blue eyes drank us in. They looked deep into me. I knew what they were saying.

'Thank you. And farewell.'

My eyes were moist. I wiped away a tear.

When I looked up, the fox had gone. I never saw it again.

In the morning the little lemon tree was dead. Every leaf was curled and brown.

'It's never grown well,' said Dad. 'And it should have. Because we planted it on Grandad's grave.'

Smelly Feat

1

'No,' screamed Dad. 'Please don't. No, no, no. Have mercy. Please, Berin, don't do it.' He dropped down on his knees and started begging.

'Very funny,' I said as I pulled off one running shoe.

Dad rolled around on the floor. 'I'm dying,' he yelled. 'I can't stand it.' He held his nose and watched me untie the other shoe.

Talk about embarrassing. He was supposed to be a grown-up man. My father. And here he was acting like a little kid in Grade Three. He always carried on like this when I came back from tennis.

My feelings were hurt. 'I can't smell anything,' I said.

'You need a nose job then,' he snorted.

My little sister Libby put her bit in. 'The fox never smells its own,' she said through a crinkled nose.

Talk about mean. I was sick of them picking on me every time I took off my shoes. I shoved my socks into my runners and stomped off to my bedroom. I threw myself down on the bed and looked around the room. Garlic was running around in her cage. I tapped the wire with my toe.

Garlic was my pet mouse. 'At least you like me,' I said.

The little mouse didn't say anything. Not so much as a squeak. In fact something strange happened. Garlic sniffed the air. Then she closed her eyes and fell fast asleep.

I jumped up and tapped the cage. Nothing. Not a movement. At first I thought she was dead but then I noticed her ribs going in and out. She was breathing.

I ran across the room to fetch Dad. But just as I reached the door I noticed Garlic sit up and sniff. She was all right. I ran back over to her. She started to totter as if she was drunk. Then she fell over and settled down into a deep sleep. I walked away and waited on the other side of the room. Garlic sat up and scampered around happily.

Something strange was going on. Every time I went

near the cage, Garlic would fall asleep. When I left she woke up. My mouse was allergic to me.

I looked down at my feet. It couldn't be. Could it? No. They weren't that bad. I put on my slippers and approached the cage. Garlic was happy. I slowly took off one slipper and held a bare foot in front of the wire.

Garlic dropped like a stone. She didn't even have time to wrinkle her nose. I put the slipper back on. Garlic sat up and sniffed happily.

This was crazy. My feet smelt so bad they could put a mouse to sleep. Just like chloroform. I had to face up to it. Even though I couldn't smell a thing, I had the strongest smelling feet in the world.

2

I went out into the back yard to look for our cat. She was licking herself in the sun 'Here, Fluffer,' I said. She looked up as I pushed a bare foot into her face.

Her eyes turned to glass and she fell to the ground. Fast asleep. I put the slipper back on my foot and Fluffer sprang to life. With a loud 'meow', she hurtled off over the fence.

This was crazy. My feet worked on a cat.

A loud noise filled the air. Barking. It was that rotten dog down the street. Its name was Ohda and it barked all night. 'Ruff, ruff, ruff.' On and on and on. Most nights you couldn't get to sleep for it barking.

I smiled to myself. This was my big chance. I left my slippers on the porch and set off down the street. Ohda was a huge dog. An Alsatian. She growled and snapped and tore at the wire gate with her teeth. I was glad she couldn't get out. I approached the gate carefully and held out a foot. Ohda stopped barking and sniffed. Her eyes watered. She held her feet up to her nose and rubbed at it furiously with her paws. Then she rolled over on her back and whimpered.

The poor dog was suffering terribly. It was just like Dad rolling around on the floor and pretending he was dying. Suddenly Ohda yelped and squealed. The huge dog bolted off into the far corner of the yard and sat staring at me as if I was a monster. Ohda was terrified.

3

I walked home slowly and thoughtfully. My feet could put a mouse to sleep. And a cat. But not a dog. They weren't powerful enough for dogs. 'Dogs must be too big,' I said to myself.

Dad sat on the sofa watching the TV. As soon as I entered the room he screwed up his nose. 'Oh, Berin,' he groaned. 'Those feet are foul. Go and have a shower.'

I couldn't take any more. The world was against me. Dad was picking on me again. Garlic had fallen asleep. Fluffer had collapsed into a coma. Ohda had been reduced to a whimper. Even the animals didn't like me.

I rushed out of the house and slammed the door. I headed down the street without caring where I was going. Tears pricked behind my eyes. I loved animals. It wasn't fair. I was born with smelly feet. I couldn't help it.

After a bit I found myself at the beach. The tide was in and a little river of sea water cut Turtle Island off from the shore. I felt a little better. Turtle Island. My favourite spot. And in three months time, in November, my favourite thing was going to happen.

Old Shelly, one of the last of the South Pacific sea turtles, would haul herself up the beach to lay her eggs. If you were lucky and knew where to look you might be there when she arrived. Every year, on the twentieth of November, she came to lay her eggs.

Once there had been hundreds of turtles crawling up the beach every summer. But people caught them for soup. And stole the eggs. Now there were hardly any turtles left. I knew where she would come ashore. But I didn't tell anybody. Not a soul. Old Shelly was two hundred years old. I couldn't stand it if anything happened to her. Or her eggs.

Seagulls swooped down and formed a swarming flock on the sand. I walked towards them. As I went they started to collapse. One after another they fell over and littered the beach like feathery corpses.

Even the seagulls were passing out when they smelt my feet. The smile fell from my face. I had to clean my feet. I strode into the salty water and headed for Turtle Island. The sand swirled between my toes. The water was cold and fresh.

I looked behind me and saw the gulls waking. They flew and squawked, alive and wide awake.

Some of them followed me to the other side. They scuttled along the sand and approached me as I left the water. Nothing happened. The gulls didn't fall asleep. The sea had washed away the smell. The animals of the world were safe again.

4

I looked along the beach and frowned. Footsteps in the sand. They walked off along the shore into the distance. I always felt as if Turtle Island was my own special place. I didn't like anyone else going there. There are some cruel people in the world and the fewer that knew about Old Shelly the better.

I followed the footsteps along for about a kilometre. They finally led into a huge sea cave. I silently made my way inside and edged around the deep pools that sank into the rocky floor. It was a favourite crayfishing spot.

Three kids were lowering a craypot into the water. It was Horse and his gang. They didn't see me at first. 'Empty,' said Horse. 'Not one rotten cray. I bet someone's been here and nicked 'em.'

Horse was a real big kid. All the members of his gang were big. Greg Baker was his closest mate. 'Just

wait till November the third,' he said. 'Turtle soup.'
They all laughed.

'And turtle omelette,' said Horse.

I couldn't believe what I was hearing. They planned
to catch Old Shelly. After two hundred years of
swimming free in the sea the grand old creature
would end up as soup. It wasn't right. My head
swam. I jumped out from behind the rock.

'You can't do it,' I screamed. 'There's hardly any
turtles left. She might even be the last one.'

They all turned and looked at me. 'A spy,' said
Horse.

'Berin Jackson,' said his mate Greg Baker. 'The
little turtle lover. What a dag.'

The other kid there was nicknamed Thistle. I didn't
notice him edging his way behind me. I was too mad
to notice anything.

'You can't hurt that turtle,' I screamed. 'It's
protected.'

'Who's going to stop us?' sneered Greg Baker.

'Me,' I yelled. 'I'll tell my Dad.'

They thought about that for a bit. 'We wouldn't
hurt the turtle, would we?' sneered Horse.

'Nah,' said the other two.

I knew they were lying. And they knew that I knew

they were lying. But there was nothing I could do.
You can't dob someone in for something they might
do.

'Get him,' yelled Horse.

Thistle grabbed me from behind. The other two
held one leg each. They lifted me into the air.

'Let me go, you scumbags,' I shouted. There were
tears in my eyes. I tried to blink them back as they
swung me higher and higher. I struggled and kicked
but they were too strong for me.

Suddenly they let go. I flew through the air and
splashed into the deep water. I sank down, down,
down and then spluttered up to the surface. I spat
out salt water and headed for the rocky shore. The
gang were already leaving. They laughed and shouted
smart comments back at me.

5

It was the worst day of my life. Animals fainting at
my feet. Tossed into the water by a bunch of bullies.
And now, Horse's gang were going to try and catch
Old Shelly.

I walked home along the beach, shivering and wet.
I thought about that turtle. Two hundred years ago

she hatched out on this very beach. Her mother would have laid scores of eggs. When the tide was right the babies would have hatched and struggled towards the water. Seagulls would have pounced and eaten most of them. In the sea, fish would have gobbled others.

Old Shelly might have been the only one to live. And for the last two hundred years she had swum and survived. And now Horse and his rotten gang were going to catch her.

There was nothing I could do. If I told Dad about the gang they would just lie and say I made it up. I knew those kids. They were in my class at school. I had tangled with them before. They were too strong for me. I couldn't handle them on my own.

Or could I?

I suddenly had an idea. Three months. I had three months to get ready before Old Shelly began to lumber ashore and dig a hole for her eggs. Three months should be enough. It might work. It just might work. I might just be able to save the turtle if I used my brains.

And my feet.

6

That night I emptied out my sock drawer. I had six pairs of blue socks. Mum bought them at a sale. I slipped one pair on my feet. Then I put on my running shoes. After that I struggled into my pyjamas. I could just get my feet through the legs without taking off my shoes.

I hopped into bed. But I felt guilty. I pulled back the blankets and looked at the sheets. The runners were making the sheets dirty. I jumped out of bed and crept down to the kitchen. I found two clear plastic bags. Just right. I pulled them over my shoes and fastened them around my ankles with elastic bands. Terrific. I pulled up the covers and fell asleep.

I had a wonderful dream.

In the morning I faced my next problem. The shower. As soon as the coast was clear I nipped into the bathroom and locked the door. I didn't want my little sister Libby to see me. She would dob for sure.

The shower was on the wall over the bath. I put in the plug and turned on the shower. When the bath was full I took off my pyjamas and lowered myself in. But I left my feet hanging out over the edge. I couldn't let my running shoes get wet. And I couldn't take them off. Otherwise my plan would fail.

That night before bed I took a pair of clean blue socks out of the cupboard. I went outside and rubbed them in the dirt. Then I threw them in the wash basket. That way Mum would think I had worn the socks that day and she wouldn't get suspicious.

Every morning and every night I did the same thing. I wondered if it would work. I planned to go for three months without taking off my shoes.

It was a diabolical plan. I wouldn't have done it normally. Not for anything. But this was different. I had to save Old Shelly from the gang. And smelly feet were my only weapon.

If my feet could send a cat to sleep after only one day, imagine what they could do after three months. Three months in the same socks and the same shoes. Three months without taking off my running shoes. What an idea. It was magnificent. I smiled to myself. I really hoped it would work.

7

Well, it was difficult. You can imagine what Mum would have said if she'd known I was wearing my shoes to bed.

140

And I had to stop Libby from finding out too.

Every night for three months I went to bed with my runners on. And every night I dirtied a pair of socks outside and put them in the wash. Mum and Dad didn't suspect anything. Although I did have a couple of close calls.

One day Mum said, 'Your socks don't smell like they used to, Berin. You must be washing your feet a lot more.' I just smiled politely and didn't say anything.

I also had problems at school with the Phys. Ed. teacher. I had to forge a note to get out of football and gym. 'These corns are taking a long time to heal,' he said to me one day. I just smiled and limped off slowly.

Three months passed and still I hadn't taken off my shoes or socks once. I hoped and hoped that my plan would work. I knew that Horse's gang were planning to catch Old Shelly. They sniggered every time I walked past them at school.

Finally the day came. November the twentieth. High tide was at half past four. After school. Old Shelly wouldn't arrive until the top of the tide. And the gang wouldn't be able to do anything while they were in school.

All went well in the morning. But after lunch it was different. I walked into the class and sat down in my seat. The day was hot. Blowflies buzzed in the sticky air. Mr Lovell sat at his desk and wiped his brow. I looked around. There were three empty seats.

Horse and his mates weren't there.

They were wagging school. And I knew where they were. Down the beach. Waiting for Old Shelly.

I went cold all over. What if Old Shelly came in early? What if I was wrong about the tides? Turtle soup. I couldn't bear to think about it.

'Mr Lovell,' I yelled. 'I have to go home. I forgot something. Horse is after Old Shelly.'

All the kids looked at me. They thought I was crazy. Mr Lovell frowned. He didn't like anyone calling out without putting up their hand.

'Don't be silly, Berin,' he growled. 'We aren't allowed to let students go home without their parents' permission.'

'But I have to go,' I yelled. 'Old Shelly is . . .'

Mr Lovell interrupted. He was angry. 'Sit down, boy, and behave yourself.'

'You don't understand . . .' I began.

'I understand that you'll be waiting outside the principal's office if you don't be quiet,' he said.

142

I sat down. It was useless. Kids don't have any power. They just have to do what they're told.

Or do they?

8

I looked at my feet. I looked at the running shoes and socks that hadn't been changed for three months. I bent down and undid the laces. Then I pulled off my shoes and socks.

I stepped out into the aisle. In bare feet.

The room suddenly grew silent. The hairs stood up on the back of my neck. I looked at my feet. Long black nails curled out of my putrid toes. Slimy, furry skin was coated with blue sock fuzz. Swollen veins ran like choked rivers under the rancid flesh. The air seemed to ripple and shimmer with an invisible stench.

I sniffed. Nothing. I couldn't smell a thing. But the others could.

The blowflies were first to go. They fell from the ceiling like rain. They dropped to the floor without so much as a buzz.

Mr Lovell jumped as if a pin had been stuck into him. Then he slumped on his desk. Asleep. A crumpled heap of dreams. The class collapsed together. They just keeled over as if they had breathed a deadly gas.

They were alive. But they slept and snored. Victims of my fetid feet.

I wish I could say that there were smiles on their lips. But there weren't. Their faces were screwed up like sour cabbages.

9

I ran out of the room and across the school yard. The caretaker was emptying a rubbish bin into the burner. He dropped the bin and flopped unconscious to the ground as I passed.

My three month smell was powerful. It could work in the open at a distance of ten metres. Horse and his gang wouldn't have a chance. They wouldn't even get near me.

But I had to hurry. If Old Shelly came early ... I couldn't bear to think about it.

The beach bus was pulling up at the kerb. I had one dollar with me. Just enough. I jumped onto the bus steps.

'Turtle Island, please,' I said to the driver.

He didn't answer. He was fast asleep in his seat with the engine still ticking over. I looked along the row of seats. All the passengers were snoring their heads off. I had gassed the whole bus.

'Oh no,' I said. I jumped off the bus and headed for the beach. The quickest way was straight through the shopping mall.

I didn't really want to run barefooted through the town but this was an emergency. I passed a lady on a bike. She fell straight asleep, still rolling along the road. The bike tottered and then crashed into a bush.

This was terrible. No one could come near me without falling asleep. I ran over to help her but her eyes were firmly closed. The best thing I could do was to get away from her as quickly as possible.

10

I jogged into the shopping mall. People fell to the ground in slumbering waves as I approached. I stopped and stared around.

The street was silent. Hundreds of people slept on the footpaths and in the shops. A policeman snored in the middle of the road. I felt as if I was the only person in the world who was awake.

Suddenly I felt lonely. And sad.

But then I thought of Old Shelly. That poor, helpless turtle dragging its ancient shell up the beach. To the waiting Horse and his cooking pot.

I ran on. My heart hammered. My knees knocked. My feet fumed. 'Old Shelly,' I said. 'I'm coming, I'm coming, I'm coming.'

I pounded on and on, not stopping for the people around me as they fell to the ground like leaves tumbling in autumn.

At last I reached the beach. The tide was in. A strong current cut me off from Turtle Island. A flock of seagulls flew overhead. They plummeted to the ground reminding me of planes that had lost their pilots.

My feet still worked. They were as powerful as ever.

I gazed at the swiftly running water. I peered along the beach for a boat. There was none. I looked at my foul feet. If only I could fly. On the wind I thought I heard wicked laughter. 'Old Shelly,' I mumbled. 'I'm coming.' I plunged into the sea and waded towards the island.

My toes sank into the sand. I could feel the grains scouring my skin. Washing away at three months of muck. The water was clear and cold and salty. On and on I struggled through the cleansing stream. Splashing. Jumping. Crying. Until I reached the other side.

The seagulls scampered around my feet. They were awake. They didn't even yawn.

11

I looked down at my lily-white toes. They were spotless. The water had stolen their strength. Three months of saving my smell. Gone. Scrubbed away by the salt and the sand.

There was no sign of the three bullies. But I knew where to find them. I staggered up to the top of a huge sand dune and stared along the beach. There they were. And there in the clear blue water was a moving shadow. Old Shelly.

Horse and his mates hadn't seen her. There was still a chance. I plunged down the dune towards them, yelling and screaming. Trying to distract them from their search.

It worked. They turned around and watched me approach. I had to draw them off. Once they saw the turtle they would know which part of the beach she was on. Even if Old Shelly escaped they would dig around and find the eggs.

I knew it was no use arguing with them. They wouldn't listen. I had to say something mean.

'Bird brain,' I said weakly to Horse. I felt silly. It didn't come out right. It wasn't tough. I bunched up my fists. 'Get off this island,' I ordered.

'Who's going to make us?' jeered Horse.

'Me,' I said.

I felt very small. They were real big kids. They walked towards me with snarling faces.

I turned and ran.

'Get him.' They pelted after me. I scrambled up the sand dune and along the top. I felt them panting behind me. The sandy ground turned to rock. It cut my bare feet. They hurt like crazy. I slowed down to a hobble. My toes were bleeding. It was no use. The gang had me trapped.

I turned and faced the gang. Behind them, way below, I could see Old Shelly hauling herself over the sand. They hadn't seen her. Yet.

Thistle circled around me. They closed in. I tried to find something to defend myself. There was nothing. I put my hands in my pocket in a desperate search. My fingers found something useful.

'Get back,' I yelled. 'Or I'll use these.'

Horse laughed out loud. 'We're not scared of a pair of ...'

He never finished. He crashed to the ground like a tree falling. The others followed. They were fast asleep on the sand. I held my putrid socks in the air. Boy, were they powerful.

12

I put the socks near the sleeping bullies. Then I walked down to the beach.

Old Shelly was digging a hole with her flippers. Slowly, painfully, she dug and dug and dug. She was helpless. 'Don't worry, girl,' I said. 'I won't hurt you.'

I sat a little way off and watched the miracle. I watched the eggs drop like beads from a broken necklace. The sun sank into the sea, lighting the old turtle with gold.

I watched as Old Shelly covered the eggs and then crawled back towards the shore. Just as she reached the edge she turned. And nodded her head as if to thank me.

'Think nothing of it,' I said. 'Your eggs are safe now. I'll see you next year.'

I have to admit there was a tear in my eye as I watched her sink under the water and swim out beneath the silvery arms of the rippling moonbeams.

I went back and fetched the socks. I threw them in the sea and waited. In no time at all, Horse and his mates started to stir. They sat up and peered into the darkness. They couldn't work it out. It was light when they had fallen asleep. They didn't know where the sun had gone.

Suddenly Horse gave an enormous scream. He ran for it. The others followed him, belting along the sand as if a demon was after them. They thought I had strange powers. I guess if you think about it, they were right in a funny sort of way.

I walked slowly home.

A nasty thought entered my mind. What if Horse found more members for his gang? What if they came back to wait for Old Shelly next November?

I was worried. Then I chuckled and spoke to myself. 'If I start going to bed with my shoes on tonight,' I said, 'my feet ought to be pretty strong by this time next year.'

hotnews@puffin

Hot off the press!

You'll find all the latest exclusive Puffin news here

Where's it happening?

Check out our author tours and events programme

Best-sellers

What's hot and what's not? Find out in our charts

E-mail updates

Sign up to receive all the latest news
straight to your e-mail box

Links to the coolest sites

Get connected to all the best author web sites

Book of the Month

Check out our recommended reads

www.puffin.co.uk

Read more in Puffin

For complete information about books available from Puffin – and Penguin – and how to order them, contact us at the appropriate address below. Please note that for copyright reasons the selection of books varies from country to country.

www.puffin.co.uk

In the United Kingdom: Please write to Dept EP, Penguin Books Ltd,
Bath Road, Harmondsworth, West Drayton, Middlesex UB7 ODA

In the United States: Please write to Penguin Putnam Inc., P.O. Box 12289,
Dept B, Newark, New Jersey 07101–5289 or call 1–800–788–6262

In Canada: Please write to Penguin Books Canada Ltd,
10 Alcorn Avenue, Suite 300, Toronto, Ontario M4V 3B2

In Australia: Please write to Penguin Books Australia Ltd,
P.O. Box 257, Ringwood, Victoria 3134

In New Zealand: Please write to Penguin Books (NZ) Ltd,
Private Bag 102902, North Shore Mail Centre, Auckland 10

In India: Please write to Penguin Books India Pvt Ltd,
11 Panscheel Shopping Centre, Panscheel Park, New Delhi 110 017

In the Netherlands: Please write to Penguin Books Netherlands bv,
Postbus 3507, NL–1001 AH Amsterdam

In Germany: Please write to Penguin Books Deutschland GmbH,
Metzlerstrasse 26, 60594 Frankfurt am Main

In Spain: Please write to Penguin Books S. A., Bravo Murillo 19,
1° B, 28015 Madrid

In Italy: Please write to Penguin Italia s.r.l.,
Via Felice Casati 20, I–20124 Milano

In France: Please write to Penguin France S. A.,
17 rue Lejeune, F–31000 Toulouse

In Japan: Please write to Penguin Books Japan, Ishikiribashi Building,
2–5–4, Suido, Bunkyo-ku, Tokyo 112

In South Africa: Please write to Longman Penguin Southern Africa (Pty) Ltd,
Private Bag X08, Bertsham 2013